Waiting for Christmas

By

Pat Simmons

This novel is a work of fiction. References to real events, organizations, or places are used in a fictional context.

Any resemblances to actual persons, living or dead, are entirely coincidental.

Special thanks to:

The Lord has inspired me to write meaningful Christmas stories to remind us of Jesus' purpose on earth, and I'm thankful for the opportunity to be a part of His writing ministry.

Freelance editor Chandra Sparks Splond for going above and beyond with assisting me to polish Ciara and Sterling story.

My author friends who support my work.

The many book clubs who invite me to their meetings and post thoughtful reviews.

Beta readers Stacey Jefferson and Darlene Simmons.

Virtual assistant Jackie Roberts.

My husband Kerry Simmons and our daughter Simi Simmons.

Son, Jared Simmons, who debuts as one of the cover models for this book.

And the many others who pray for me when I'm in my writing cave.

Praises for Pat Simmons

5.0 OUT OF 5 STARS WOOOOOOOOOW.

Just when you think that it can't get any better.... Pat Simmons exceeded my expectations. This book is exceptional. It touched me in so many ways and I could really relate to Robyn because she reminded me of myself. I could just picture her putting her fist on her hips and the sassy way that she would respond to Derek. The proposal was the highlight in the book for me. The reference to Job sent chills over me. —Reader Ceisha Barrett on *Couple by Christmas*

4.0 out of 5 stars Christmas Stories

Pat has a way with scriptures in her stories. I wonder which comes first the scriptures or the stories. I read the Gifts from God series and enjoyed both books, but Prayers Answered by Christmas was my favorite. I love the innocence of the children. Well done Pat. I look forward to Coy's story. She needs some love from God too. —Amazon Reader on *Prayers Answered by Christmas*

5.0 out of 5 stars Beautiful Story of Love and Family

Pat Simmons has written a story showcasing the power of love and family. I smiled and cried as Daniel and Saige's story progressed. Pat handles a very emotional issue beautifully and reminds us that God's will is always perfect, even when we want Him to do things differently. I will think about this story for a while as I meditate on how He does all things well. Are you looking for a Christmas story that will warm your heart? You don't need to look any further than *Christmas Greetings* by Pat Simmons. Great job Pat, if I could, I would give a rating of 6 stars. —Reader Leslie Hudson

Chapter One

Sterling Price was the epitome of magnificence. He commanded the lobby of Ciara Summers' office with a bold presence and gentle smile. She couldn't look away as his features drew her in.

A thick, untamed black beard.

Unblemished, rich milk chocolate skin.

A perfect combination.

His brown suit—a rarity these days—set him apart. Either it was tailored-made for him, or he was the spokesman for the brand. Again, perfection.

The philanthropist was nothing like she had envisioned, not that Ciara had conjured up an image of him at all. For the past couple of weeks, Mr. Price's weekly contributions to Help 100 Families—a Christmas initiative that she spearheaded—had been like clockwork, online and via phone.

Whew. Ciara was having a fan moment. She dismissed it. His eyes danced as a smile tugged at his lips. Bright white teeth captivated her. *Hmph.* Good dental hygiene made her take a double look every time.

"Mr. Price, I'm Ciara. How can I help you today?" she asked in a professional tone to keep from blushing. *No drooling.*

"Please, call me Sterling." He took a step forward and towered over Ciara Summers' five-feet-six inches. Close enough for her to notice his brown eyes, as clear and unblemished as the marbles in her father's collection. "I'm here to give my dona-tion."

Her nostrils took the liberty of inhaling his cologne. A blend of citrus and woodsy.

Don't get distracted. "And we'll gladly accept it for our fam-ilies on the list. I apologize our website was down last time, but it has since been corrected, so your donations are safe. Sorry you had to make a special trip."

He studied her. *Why?* "I find this trip very rewarding."

Her gaze captured his slow grin as he slipped one hand into his pants pocket and came out empty. *No check?*

"Since you've assisted me before with my donation, why break our tradition?" He shrugged off his coat as if he were stay-ing.

Tradition? They did not have one. She had only spoken once to this handsome man—although she didn't know that at the time—over the phone.

As a licensed social worker, Ciara was honored to be ap-pointed to the board for the annual fundraiser. Two months out of the year, this office was her hangout. Her background al-lowed her to bring awareness to the plight of others who could be experiencing life's hardships in plain sight and solicit funds on their behalf. Helping with contributions was part of her job description.

Ciara didn't hide her amusement. She hadn't had an instant attraction to a man since...she wracked her brain...a blind date a few years ago, but by the second date, Ciara's attraction fizzled.

She cleared her throat and smiled. "Okay. If you take out your phone and have a seat," pointing to the lounge area in the lobby, "I can walk you through it."

Sterling made a confident stride to a nook where two over-sized chairs, a leather sofa, and a glass coffee table awaited him.

Ciara exchanged glances with the volunteer receptionist, who was in her fifties. Terri Davis fanned herself as if Sterling's presence had triggered a hot flash.

Right? Ciara mouthed. Sterling had them captivated.

Terri recovered first, reminding Ciara the man came to see her.

Remain professional, Ciara's mind coaxed while her maternal time clock shouted, "Girl, flirt. Don't you want a husband? Children?"

Not right at this moment.

As she took the seat next to him to walk him through the online process, Ciara collected her thoughts to keep from swooning. As he tapped on his phone, she admired his trimmed nails. Clean nails and white teeth said a lot about a person—a neat, healthy lifestyle or, on the downside, self-absorbed.

"Log on to <u>Help100Families' website</u> where the St. Louis newspaper has featured this week's families in crises," she said, as if he had forgotten the process after his previous contributions. So far, twenty families had been profiled with eighty more to go with six weeks left in the year.

Sterling tapped his phone, and it came to life with a wallpaper of two women smiling.

"They're pretty." She gestured at the screen.

"Thanks. My younger sisters."

"I have two sisters too." Ciara chuckled.

He rested his phone on the table and gave her his full attention. "That's two things we have in common."

Along with a million other families that had more than one daughter. His stare dared her to disagree, so Ciara held her breath and didn't.

"What families would you like to support this week? We're featuring cases fifteen through eighteen."

He rubbed his chin, smoothing the hairs of his beard. Sterling propped his elbows on his knees and leaned closer. "Tell me about them."

"May I?" Ciara asked for permission before she tapped on his screen, then zoomed out to view the text on the cases. "Here are their profiles if you want to read them."

"Nah. I like listening to your voice, Ciara." He grinned. "Is it okay to call you by your first name?"

"Yes," she faintly heard herself say as her heart pounded loudly in her ears. His smooth baritone voice had awakened her senses.

This man is not flirting with you, her mind chimed. *Stay focused.* "Case fifteen is a single mother with a small son with autism. She feels lost in the system. Most of the year, they're homeless... During November and December, she is staying with her sister who has three children of her own... She is asking for socks and coats for when they have to return to the streets..."

He looked bewildered. "Why can't she continue living with her sister?"

Ciara swallowed back her sorrow and glanced up. "Sounds like both mothers are struggling. We don't know the situation that prohibits her from staying there permanently."

Sterling's eyes seemed to be waiting for hers to meet his.

"That's sad." His expression reminded her of a handsome five-year-old. Emphasis on *handsome.* "No toys?"

"Toys don't always make the perfect gift," she explained.

Possessing a master's in social work, Ciara witnessed first-hand what a two-hundred-word write-up couldn't capture. Most families wanted to stay together with or without shelter.

"Of the thousands of families nominated through social agencies for Help 100 Families, many ask for the bare necessities."

"Would you pick case number fifteen?"

Ciara shook her head. "Sorry, I'm not here to lead you to one scenario over another. It's against the rules to influence the donor. Follow your heart."

"I understand. That's okay." He squinted at his screen. "Every week, I find it harder to choose. That one right there," he said, tapping on his screen, "is toying with my emotions."

He scrolled down his phone and read the next case himself. *"Case sixteen is a disabled grandmother who is rearing her three grandchildren and has no washer or dryer because of... It's unsafe to send the girls, eight and ten, to the Laundromat, which is blocks away. The neighborhood is known for drug activity and... Any amount to help buy another washer would be appreciated. A dryer would be a bonus, because they are using space heaters."*

Sterling was silent. Ciara allowed him the space to reflect on his selections.

Every year, the one hundred cases tugged at people's hearts, and every year, Ciara prayed that each family would get their requests fulfilled.

While Sterling was deep in thought, Ciara observed him. Slight dimple. Flawless skin—not a razor mishap in sight—and his black hair, thick and wavy. She was about to admire his lashes—a wasted endowment on men—but glanced away so he wouldn't catch her staring.

"The woman's practical, and that's humbling." His voice startled her.

She nodded "Yes. Grandmothers are sometimes the safety pin keeping families together." She fumbled with her fingers to mask her nervousness and urge to nudge him to pick the grandma.

No, you don't. Ciara never broke those rules—ever. Donations had to be made under the sole discretions of the giver without any influence from the staff.

He read the last two featured profiles. "*Case number eighteen is a twenty-seven-year-old mother of five who had been in an abusive situation after her husband was released from prison... Without a car, coats for the children ages one, three, seven, eleven, and twelve would help when they walk to the bus stop to flee the violence when the father drinks.*"

"Whew." Sterling scratched his neck. "This isn't easy."

His compassion was attractive. Overpowering. Ciara felt tempted to rub soothing circles on his back.

Closing his eyes, Sterling rubbed his forehead as if to ward off a pending headache. "All of them are asking for so little but need so much. Okay. Three hundred dollars to each family."

Ciara's heart wanted to belt a soprano note as if this man had professed his love and had given her the rock to back it up. But she wasn't a singer.

"That's twelve hundred dollars and very generous, Mr. Price." She kept her excitement at bay. His last donation of two hundred dollars was split between two families. But there were other cases donors had overlooked. A few from the previous week had yet to receive fifty bucks. Those were the ones Ciara tracked.

Hoping.

Praying for someone to notice.

And if no one did, Ciara stepped in and gave out of her pocket.

"I wish I could do more."

"That's how I feel every day. As a regular contributor, perhaps you might want to consider adopting a family for a year."

He shook his head. "I like spreading the blessings to as many families as I can."

"That's sweet," Ciara heard herself saying.

"You're going to make me blush, Miss Summers," he said, pausing, "unless you're a Mrs. who doesn't wear a ring or have plans to become a blessed man's Mrs.?" Sterling didn't blink, neither was he subtle with his scoping.

"It's Miss—for now." Although flattered, Ciara refused to take the bait. Not that she wasn't available. She wasn't interested in playing games, and that seemed to be the only options in dating lately. "Again, on behalf of Help 100 Families, thank you."

Sterling checked his watch. "Since I've done my good deed for the day, maybe we can celebrate over lunch, if your significant other wouldn't mind." His smile dared her to say no.

Terri, who had been quiet as a listening device, suddenly had a fit of fake coughs.

"No to a boyfriend, estranged husband, fiancée, or lunch. Sorry." Not the status Ciara wanted at thirty-three, but so be it. She stood and guided him across the lobby to the door. It was time for their goodbyes.

Even if she wasn't a rule breaker, Ciara knew nothing about Sterling Price except he had no problem parting ways with his money, and he adored his two sisters. That didn't mean he wasn't a charmer with a dark past.

Folding her hands, she lifted her chin, and in her sweetest tone, she excused herself to return to work. Sterling hadn't moved. If he did, the door would have creaked. Ciara kept her strut steady. She wasn't going to change her mind.

Maybe at another time, place, or season that wouldn't jeopardize his contributions.

WHAT DID YOU EXPECT her to say?

Sterling slid behind the wheel of his Jeep, adjusted his Fedora, and headed back to Every Dime We Spend, his thriving Internet-based marketing company. "Yes, would have been like winning tickets to the World Series." He checked his rearview mirror.

Since she said no, Sterling had to plan his next visit. He would never give online again.

Stalker—absolutely not.

Harmless—definitely.

Interested—very.

It was refreshing for a woman to tell him no. Usually, when a lady learned he was the owner of a startup company, her first questions were whether he had turned a profit, how much money was in his bank, and what his stocks traded for on the New York Stock Exchange. Not to mention his credit limit. Sterling was their prey.

Ciara wasn't chasing him, and that piqued his curiosity.

Sterling chuckled to himself. Without much thought, he had chosen Help 100 Families for his end-of-the-year charitable contributions. His first online experience had been seamless. The second time, the website was down. That was bad for any business.

He had called the agency and eventually was transferred to Ciara. She had no idea her voice had drawn him in—it was between soft and sweet, sultry, and alluring. Ciara had apologized for the inconvenience.

She kept their conversation going while she troubleshot the issue, sharing how much families depended on the program. In no time, Ciara realized the problem had been on their site and alerted her tech team right away.

As important as the donations were, Ciara didn't become flustered. Sterling had been a bit disappointed when she processed his payment, and there was nothing else for them to discuss.

He wasn't ready to let their brief interaction go, so he checked the website to find out more about her and discovered she was beautiful and one of four board of directors for Help 100 Families.

He had almost spilled his coffee on his crisp white shirt as she seemed to stare back at him. Instead, his keyboard had suffered the injury. After the mindless cleanup, Sterling had to see for himself if the woman on the company's website was Photoshopped or as pretty in person.

Website crashes, connectivity, or other issues were never a good thing, especially for an ecommerce business. His company matched Black consumers with Black businesses in the local St. Louis area. The startup that began eight years earlier turned a profit in its fourth year and never looked back except to give back to the community.

Who knew Help 100 Families would spark a need in him for companionship—no setups from his sisters or his mother? Just a chance meeting where there might be a hint of an attraction.

Sterling saw Ciara blush, and her full lips curved upward into a tease. His heart rhythm skipped. Her mesmerizing slanted brown eyes hinted of Asian mixed with her rich Black ancestry.

Ciara's deep blue blouse complemented her rich jet-black hair. When she appeared, Sterling did his best to act reserved and not to be affected by her appearance. Not an easy task when the brown beauty reminded him of pure honey. If he wasn't at her place of employment, he would have thought Ciara had left an all-day beauty spa.

Sterling's attraction remained steady in Ciara's presence while she masked her curiosity about him. Returning to work would prove to be a challenge after a glimpse of Ciara Summers.

He parked in his assigned space in front of the two-story brick building with an archway entrance that was nestled in the historic Mid-Town neighborhood. Once inside, he hiked the stairs to the second floor, which housed his dream. Sterling unlocked his office door and flipped on the lights.

"Hey, where did you go, man?" Dray Blakely, his co-founder, was on his heels.

"Ran an errand." A beautiful one.

"In a suit. I guess you dressed to impress. Bring in the dollars and cents and you can play dress up all day." He bobbed his clean-shaven head.

Sterling ignored the ribbing. When he had business meetings or lunches, Sterling represented with a suit and tie, Dray made a big deal about nothing.

"On a serious note, we need to go over pricing for the potential clients' contracts. Got time?"

"Yep." Sterling slipped off his suit coat, then joined his friend at the round table by his desk. All thoughts of Ciara Summers were pushed to the side—no, folded up nice and neat until he could retrieve them in his private moments. He couldn't wait.

"I was on a conference call with Ken and the guys."

Kenneth Dixon and four other Black men graduated from college with Dray and Sterling. Some had worked in Corporate America after college, but now they were successful entrepreneurs.

"Yeah?" Sterling glanced up at Dray. "What's up?"

"Kenneth's talking smack. He and his company have pledged ten thousand dollars in charitable contributions by this

Christmas season, and they're daring anyone to come close. He even said if any of us meet him at the ten thousand level, he'll match it." Dray grunted. "Show-off."

"Actually, that's generous." Sterling rubbed his jaw in thought. "We're all small business owners. Last year, Kenneth's transportation company gave eight thousand in contributions to make the number one spot, and we came in third place at forty-five hundred." He shrugged. "Not bad."

Dray pounded his fist on the table and twisted his lips as if he had tasted something sour. "I want to come in first place and match his giving."

Sterling squinted. "Slow down. This is a friendly agreement for Black entrepreneurs to give back to our community. Not a competition. I gave twelve hundred dollars earlier to Help 100 Families. Happy now?"

"Only if we beat KenDixon Logistics."

His friend and business partner was trying Sterling's patience. There was a reason Sterling was the chief financial officer of the company and Dray's strength was chief operating officer. Sterling was a hawk when it came to tracking the money going out and coming in.

He would not allow Dray to give away the kitchen sink for the sake of winning. This wasn't a bet. Charitable contributions weren't meant to be played like the Missouri Lottery that Dray often won.

Sterling needed to take his own counsel around Ciara Summers. He gave more today than he intended, but Sterling knew how to adjust his next contributions.

Chapter Two

C iara laughed at her baby sister's antics. "Bet you wished you hadn't done that. What's wrong with you?"

The youngest at twenty-seven, Amber had snatched the white onion off Ciara's cutting board and inhaled. Batting her lashes, Amber stumbled backward at the assault of her senses. She released the onion to Ciara and Jessica's amusement.

The three sisters manned their mother's kitchen to prepare Thanksgiving dishes ahead of schedule while their parents hung Christmas decorations in the living room. Recovering, Amber rolled the offending vegetable back to Ciara. "Whew. I wanted to make sure this wasn't an imposter. You're cutting onions and smiling? Who does that?"

"Was I?" Ciara kept a blank face and continued her task.

"It was definitely a smile. Your lips curved up. You had a slight smirk too," Amber said, rubbing her eyes from the onion's irritant with her arm. "You were probably about to hum any minute."

"It's either a dude, dog, or dress," Jessica said, the oldest at thirty-five. She was married and the mother of two small children.

Ciara made sure to hide her amusement as she kept dicing. "I did see this cute miniature dog in a turtleneck sweater. That made me smile." She had to play it cool around her nosy brat sister who never lacked a date to a function. Ciara had no problem going solo to an event. Her sisters' attempts at finding Ciara plus-ones had been disastrous.

Amber lived in a fantasy world that cute guys were good guys. In Ciara's line of work, the myth was dispelled regularly. Boyfriends and husbands turned their wives, girlfriends, and children's world upside down, leaving agencies to rescue them.

Ciara was okay with not dating.

Daydreaming about it was playing it safe.

Acting upon a perceived attraction was not smart.

"*Humph.* You won't make eye contact with us, so it must be a man—a good-looking one. Come on, spill it," Amber whined. "I'm your best friend and favorite sister."

"Excuse me," Jessica said, playfully shoving Amber aside. "I'm the oldest here, and by default, the favorite. Share your holiday cheer, so we can be merry and bright."

Jessica bumped Ciara's hip. "Come on. Christmas music is serenading us from the living room. The scent of baked goods is setting the stage for the holidays. All that's needed is a special someone for you to spend the season with."

"Okay. Okay." Ciara tamed her excitement. "One of the donors to Help 100 Families came into the office today…"

Amber groaned and slumped her shoulders. "Why am I not surprised it has something to do with work? What can you tell us about this donor?"

"It was his third donation," Ciara explained.

Rolling her eyes, which were still watery from the onions, Amber rested her elbows on the counter and folded her arms. "Of course," she said, twisting her lips in disappointment, "your heart bleeds for those families."

"Yep. My prayer is that they all get something this Christmas, but I can't influence the donors."

"Girl, please. Oh, I thought you were about to tell us you met someone." Jessica gave her a side-eye.

"I did—in a way." Ciara grinned. "He was handsome, no ring on his finger, and he asked about my relationship status."

Amber squealed and high-fived Jessica, who performed an impromptu happy dance. Their baby sister became Jessica's dance partner.

"Hold up. Not so fast. I was flattered," she said, lifting her hand in a time-out motion, "but I'm not compromising my job—"

Jessica snickered. "Unless embezzlement is involved, a meaningful livelihood and a godly social life is happiness for life." She shook her head. "There's a man shortage out there." She pointed to the back door.

"Let's pretend." Amber reached for her mixing bowl and brought it closer to Ciara and her onions. "If you saw him on the street, and he asked for your number, would you consider it?"

"No. I don't talk to strangers." Ciara jutted her chin.

Amber gritted her teeth. "Work with me on this. Suppose you weren't involved with Help 100 Families, would you be interested in... What's his name?"

Ciara gave her sister a pointed stare. "You know I can't discuss—"

"She asked for a name, sis, not his bank account." Jessica double teamed Ciara. "Even I know if his donation isn't made anonymously, it's public information. We're not asking you to disclose how much he gave. All we need is a name." She looked to Amber for confirmation. "We can take it from there."

"And that's scary." Ciara scooped her onions and added them to Amber's bowl for the turkey dressing.

"The guy must be creepy." Jessica shrugged.

He had taken Ciara breath away. "Far from it. Sterling Price has a nice smile, nice eyes, build, beard—" Oops. Too late to catch herself. She had said too much.

"Sterling Price. Amber, grab your phone," Jessica ordered.

"On it." Amber reached into her pocket without cleaning her hands. The evidence was on her screen. "I'm online now."

Amber's "wows" made Ciara look. She swallowed hard so as not to drool.

Jessica wagged her finger. "The next time Mr. Price asks you out to breakfast, lunch, or a snack, say yes. If it's money you want, maybe you can charm him to up his donation."

"That's what I don't want to do."

"We're not going to let you talk yourself out of a chance to meet a man who could be your future husband." Jessica huffed.

"According to his profile, Mr. Price is a business owner. Success agrees with him. His status is single—not separated, married, divorced, or complicated," Amber sang and held the last note. "I envision fancy dinners, expensive gifts, and who knows what other perks."

"That doesn't impress me. I'm not a user or a gold digger..." She scrunched her nose, not liking manipulators.

"You can't be a gold digger if you're not after the man's money," Jessica insisted.

That was the problem. Ciara was after Sterling's money on a professional level.

She just couldn't ask for it.

"The next time you see him, promise me you won't say no to a conversation over food." Jessica rested her hand on her hip.

It was a standoff among the sisters. "I can't promise I'll say yes, either. Now, we've wasted enough time. Let's finish up in here. Sterling got my hint. Not interested."

THREE STRIKES, AND Sterling would be out if she said wasn't interested. A week later, Sterling was at the offices for Help 100 Families hoping Ciara wouldn't make it strike two.

She intrigued him. Expressions played across Ciara's face. Was she thinking of creative ways, or a different language, to say no?

Sterling pressed. "I'm asking for lunch. I'm starved. You can order whatever you want on me and talk about whatever you want—weather, pets, siblings, your Christmas list."

He waited.

"I don't think that's going to work." She shook her head, and her hair bounced from side to side.

Not the answer he had hoped for. What was it about this beauty who made him drop what he was doing at the office and take off for lunch on an unseasonably cold day? Donations were not on his mind this time.

Then it happened. Ciara gave him a smile as he rambled like a kindergartener instead of a college graduate with two degrees. He exhaled, encouraged, until she turned and disappeared down the hall. Huh?

The receptionist looked the other way. Was she embarrassed for him?

Sterling had to man up and mask his disappointment. Should he reconsider a third attempt? His father told him his mother turned him down eight times before she consented to a coffee break at their job. *Whew.* Sterling wasn't one for that much rejection.

Forget three strikes. He wouldn't ask Ciara again, and if he wanted to be petty, his money would be better appreciated elsewhere. He wasn't looking for a relationship anyway.

Liar. His heart said otherwise. Sterling yearned for a commitment that hadn't come setups from friends and family, as if they knew what he desired. His heart would recognize what he needed.

Ciara wasn't the one. As he was about to leave, she returned, pointing to her Bluetooth. "Sorry about that. I was on the phone." She pointed to her ear.

Wearing a bashful grin, Sterling exhaled. So, it wasn't bad breath or sleep in his eyes that had sent her away. "Does that mean you didn't hear a word I said?"

"Heard everything." Ciara wrestled with her coat sleeves.

Sterling took three strides to assist. She seemed surprised by his gesture but gave him a smile that could warm a cold cup of hot chocolate.

"What do you have a taste for?" Sterling asked while he admired her features.

"Mama's Kitchen, of course." She lifted her chin as if it were a given, forcing him to pay attention.

Sterling opened the door, and an arctic blast slapped him.

Ciara didn't shiver as she strutted across the street, leading the way. "They make the best beef stew, and their bread...*Mm-mm-mmmm-mmmm.*"

"Sounds like the hot brew my bones are aching for." Walking next to her, Sterling guessed her heeled boots put her height at his shoulders and he was six-feet-two.

Inside, the diner was a throwback to Sterling's childhood Christmases with a train charging on the tracks, disappearing in tunnels, and zipping by replicas of mountain towns. Another corner of the eatery held reverence to a Black nativity. Off to the side was a lounge area with a fireplace. Flames danced and beckoned patrons closer. Colorful stockings of various colors and sizes hung from the mantel.

Mama's Kitchen was designed for people to come, eat, and stay. The patrons were scattered throughout the large open space and were a mix of young and old, professionals and old-timers, Blacks, and whites. This downtown hangout needed to be on his radar and in his business listings.

Now that his senses were thawed, he inhaled a fruity scent while she placed her order first. Yes, he missed the companionship. His last date his baby sister had set up had been a disastrous one.

It's just lunch, he chided himself, but he wanted to know more about her than what the organization's website and social media stated.

Without glancing at the menu, she ordered the beef stew and biscuits. He did the same and paid for it. As they searched for seats, Ciara pulled off her cap, and her shoulder-length hair tumbled out from confinement. She removed her coat before Sterling could help. The two settled in a booth in front of a large window that faced the building where she worked. Once they made eye contact, the stare down began.

Sterling admitted he was mesmerized. "What made you change your mind about lunch?"

"You said you were treating." She shrugged and her full lips curved upward. A snicker was on standby.

That simple, huh? Ciara Summers was a tease. Sterling stretched his legs under the table and brushed against her boots. "Tell me something about you."

She glanced out the window, then tapped a manicured finger against her cheek. "I mentioned I had two sisters. I did my undergrad and graduate studies in social work at SEMO."

"Ah, Southeast Missouri State University." He paused when the server brought their trays to the table. Sterling reached for her hands. Yes, to pray, but to make a physical connection. When she consented, he asked for blessings for their food, then added, "Help us remember to feed those who are hungry. In Jesus' name. Amen."

Once Sterling sampled his dish, he saw why Ciara closed her eyes and smacked her lips. The seasoning and warmth spread through his body. "This is good."

"Yep." She lifted her brow in an I-told-you-so expression.

"Tell me more about you," he said, then enjoyed another mouthful.

"Hmmm." She tilted her head in thought. "I'm kind of boring."

"I doubt that." Sterling snickered.

"Seriously, I'm a workaholic in a sense because I'm always thinking of people and organizations that can help others in need. See, told ya—boring, but I like my job. I like seeing people blessing people. Your turn." She nodded.

He shrugged and swallowed. "I attended Arizona State University on a football scholarship. I like warm weather."

"Why did you move back to St. Louis?" She took another spoonful of her stew.

"My parents and one of my sisters are here. Danielle lives in Chicago. Plus, after one summer in Phoenix at 115 degrees, I realized all four seasons wasn't bad after all, but Tempe was good for me."

Sterling reached for the basket of biscuits at the same time as Ciara. He waited for her, then helped himself.

"In what way?" she asked, then took a bite.

"I learned life lessons. Not only did I excel in sports as a linebacker, but I also enjoyed the academics as a business major. It was outside the classroom, God showed me myself."

Ciara tilted her head and studied him, waiting for him to explain.

"Some other players and I went to an eating joint. We were stars on the field and off... and immature." He squirmed in his seat. Sterling grew uncomfortable. Disclosing his imperfections wasn't something he often shared. How long could he stall without his stew getting cold?

"Hey, I won't judge. I can't because I wouldn't be good in this profession if I did." Her smile encouraged him to go on.

He believed her. "As we were entering the place, a homeless guy sat outside the door begging for a handout." Sterling choked every time he thought about his behavior. "I should have been the example—the kind one. Instead, I followed the leader. We laughed at him and kept going. All throughout my meal, I couldn't shake the dejected look in that man's eyes. I had lost my appetite, but went through the motions of enjoying my food, you know?"

"Got it." She nodded. "Peer pressure."

"Yep, to be one of the boys." He grunted at himself being a coward back then. "When we left, he was still there. Out of the eight of us, I could feel his stare on me, but I never looked at him again." Sterling bowed his head in shame.

"When we graduated, we had matured. Five frat brothers and I made a commitment to reach back and help others. Never will I turn away or judge someone in need." Sterling paused and grinned. "We call ourselves the Mighty Six. Corporate America was a perfect training ground to learn the difference between cutthroat and honest business practices. One by one, we quit our jobs to start our own companies. As we thrived, we made good on giving back, no matter how small."

Sterling hadn't expected to bare his soul, but that moment in life sparked the conviction that drove him to this day.

Ciara's eyes misted, and she patted her chest. She choked on her words. "Thank you for sharing that with me. Wow."

They were quiet as they continued to eat. He had spoiled the mood. This was not the impression he wanted to paint.

"You're a fascinating man. I appreciate your life lesson. I would like to know more about you, but since you're a donor, what else would you like for me to know?" She gave him a teasing smile.

"Besides everything that's got you curious about me... *hm-mm*." Sterling stroked his beard. "Well, I'm the cofounder of an Internet marketing company. Business is good, and next year's projection is better. We have thirteen employees and are looking to hire more next year."

"A Black entrepreneur. I love it. It's brave, exciting, and takes faith."

"Thank you. I believe God was in the plan, and I want to live each day to impress Him, but at the end of the day, I find myself repenting."

She said nothing. Sterling didn't know where she stood on her relationship with God, but he had to put it out there. He didn't believe in converting women he wanted to date. Either they were practicing Christians or not.

"I admire your faith in God." She nodded. "Godly men are a premium. Tell me more about your business."

"Thanks." Sterling exhaled. "Our company, Every Dime We Spend, is the link between buyers and sellers. I'm sure at one time you've looked for Black products, restaurants, and services to support. Their presence could be buried under the competition. It takes more than search engine optimization to drive consumers to websites. Good content, products, services, plus consumer reviews keep everyone in business."

He paused. "Sorry. I get carried away."

"No, go on. Passion reveals a lot about a person."

"Yes." Sterling felt a connection. "It does, but I don't want to bore you."

She scrunched her nose at him. It was a cute gesture. "You're not."

If men blushed, Sterling did so before he could stop himself, then cleared his throat. "Our mission is to connect Black consumers with businesses that welcome their spending dollar and treat them with respect."

Ciara pushed her bowl aside and propped her elbows on the table. She rested her delicate chin on her linked hands and looked at him with such interest, as if she had all the time in the world for him. "I'm impressed. What happens when consumers who use your referrals aren't treated fairly?"

"If the business gets three strikes, they are removed from the database for three months. We want our businesses to be reputable. Other cities are taking notice of our service. Requests have come in from Black business owners in the Kansas City and Nashville markets. We're doing our research and crunching the numbers before we pitch how we can help them."

When Ciara grinned, her face glowed. "Maybe one day your company will reach the same status as Black millionaires like David L. Steward who lives right here."

"Billionaire," he corrected, "Mr. Steward has one of the largest Black businesses in America—Worldwide Technology. God can do it for us too."

"You'll make it. Good guys do win."

Did she wink at him, or was that his imagination? Sterling bit his bottom lip and readied himself for the challenge. "Since

I've convinced you that I'm a good guy, how about dinner outside of business hours?"

Lifting a brow, she tilted her head. "Dinner? That sounds like a date, and..."

Scratch that. Too soon. He got it. Sterling didn't want her to shut down before she opened to him. He switched the subject. "Tell me about your holiday traditions."

"It begins on Thanksgiving after dinner with a stakeout." She checked the time and began to gather her things. Sterling frowned. "A what? Stakeout?"

When Ciara chuckled; her eyes lit up. "Yep. Can't beat the bargain deals."

"Really? Sounds mysterious, Miss Summers. Do you need an accomplice?" He wiggled his eyebrows. What other facets of her life would be as adventurous?

"I've got two of them—my sisters."

Did she fake a pout? Seductive. He loved it.

"Our stakeouts are like tailgating parties. The early-bird bargains make staying up all night worth it."

He frowned. "I thought all the big stores are open on the holidays, so you don't have to do that anymore."

"The Accent Electronics chain hasn't caved in yet to that holiday craze. We start at their Bridgeton location."

Sterling cringed. "I prefer online shopping."

"Of course, you would, but," she said, wagging her finger, "you don't know what you're missing."

There was no love lost when it came to shopping, yet Sterling didn't want to miss an opportunity to get to know her and pray that Ciara was different from the other women he dated.

"I may beat you there."

Chapter Three

Before Ciara left work to enjoy her Thanksgiving vacation, she re-read case number twenty-three, which was one of those profiled in the *St. Louis Post-Dispatch* the previous Sunday.

The stepfather and his wife are raising three teenagers. Both are working part-time jobs to keep the children from going astray. The family isn't eligible for the school's breakfast and lunch program, but desperately need the nutrition for the children, two have health issues. A good Christmas for them would be anything, clothes or food like fruits and vegetables...

Ciara rubbed her eyes, removing any remnants of makeup. Why wasn't the family eligible for the school food program? If they were her caseload, Ciara would go on a Mama Bear tantrum over her cubs. When she returned to her regular office, Ciara would search the list to see which caseworker was assigned to this family.

That was enough brainpower on work for one day. Ciara closed her laptop, grabbed her things, and said good night to the few volunteers who remained. Tomorrow was a big day.

Thanksgiving began with a holiday service at church. Once the offering was taken and the benediction given, churchgoers dispersed to get home to welcome family and enjoy their dinners.

Ciara skipped breakfast so she could stuff herself with the yummy dishes at her parents'. Twenty minutes later, she parked in the driveway behind Jessica and Justin's SUV. Amber cruised to the curb seconds later.

The two walked inside together. After greeting their parents, the three sisters gathered in the kitchen to bring the serving dishes to the table.

"You two should know, I took your advice and went to lunch with Sterling." Ciara blushed as she tried to describe her impressions. "He's handsome. Humble. Honest."

"Basically, you're saying there's more to him than his money. See, told ya." Amber rolled her neck.

Jessica did a soft clap. "Excellent. I'm sure Justin would love a brother-in-law. I can't wait to meet him."

"Hold on. A forty-five-minute lunch at Mama's Kitchen doesn't equate to an engagement party."

"You're right. He would want something more upscale. So, when do you plan to see him again?" Jessica asked as if it were a given.

Tilting her head, Ciara considered giving her sisters a heads-up. "Maybe later, if he decides to show up at our stakeout."

Jessica's jaw dropped, and Amber gritted her teeth as their dad shouted from the other room.

"Daughters, please, a man's stomach should only growl so many times. Let's eat."

"Yeah, me too, Grandpa," her niece Dina whined.

Leaving her sisters speechless, Ciara led the way into the dining room, which had recently been remodeled with a rich hardwood floor, a trendy navy-blue coat of paint and new interior white shutters.

As the sisters arranged the dishes on the table, Ciara wondered whether Sterling would show up. That was asking for the impossible on Thanksgiving for football fans.

Once everyone took their seats and joined hands, Larry Summers offered the blessings. "Lord, Jesus, we thank You for our family and the food You've provided today and the many blessings and mercies You've given us year-round. Please watch over my little girls during their adventures today, in Jesus' name."

"Amen," Ciara said then snickered at her father calling twenty-seven-, thirty-three-, and thirty-five-year-old grown women his little girls.

Ciara was savoring the blend of cranberry sauce and turkey dressing to her palate when Amber gave her the side-eye. Her mischievous expression hinted that she was about to tamper with the tranquility at the table. Ciara sighed and counted down the seconds, leading up to her antics.

"I can't believe you broke the sisterhood Thanksgiving tradition. Shopping has always been just us—the Summers girls. Sorry, Justin." Amber glanced at her brother-in-law. "A plus-one has never been part of the deal."

Their father's blank expression made Ciara guess at his thoughts.

"Amber, think of it this way," Jessica said, winking, "we can interrogate him."

"Poor man," Justin mumbled as Ciara caught her sister elbowing her husband.

Their father's voice boomed. "Who is this young man?"

"Someone Ciara met at work," Amber answered.

"At least it wasn't online." Her mother scooped up a mouthful of green beans in the next breath.

Larry Summers' size made him an imposing man at the head of the table. His bark wasn't a bluff when it came to his family. Steam would emit any minute from his flared nostrils. "Either he's a fellow caseworker or a case. I don't like either scenario. Social workers don't make that much, and her cases need too much."

"I love my job, Daddy," Ciara said, sighing, "and you taught us to never look down on those in need."

"And I meant every word of it, except when it comes to providing for my daughters." He pounded his fist on the table, shaking the silverware. Her mother wrapped her hands around his hand to bring his temper down a notch.

Protective didn't begin to describe her father. Before Justin married Jessica, he couldn't make inroads with their dad. Then Justin discovered a secret weapon: his family's secret sauce for the grill. Larry was a sucker for homemade barbecue sauces.

Justin had to smother his secret recipe on ribs at two family barbecues to win Larry over. Not long afterwards, their father gave his consent for Justin to marry Jessica. Giving her father his first grandson and granddaughter kept Justin in his good graces.

"Dear, our daughter is a good judge of character. If Ciara invited this young man—" She snapped her fingers and eyed Ciara to fill in the blank.

"Sterling Price," Amber said.

"What kind of name is Sterling? What's wrong with David, Harold, or Justin?" Larry asked.

Jessica's husband looked up when his name was called and nodded his appreciation, then kept eating.

"Calm down. No one has to worry. I mentioned it, I didn't invite him. I told him it's a sisterhood thing—sort of."

But what if he did come? That would wow her.

Larry exhaled. "Should have said that at first. Now, can someone pass that sweet potato pie?"

To Ciara's relief, the grandchildren took center stage. After dinner, the sisters cleared the table, loaded the dishwasher, and put the food away, except for the makings of sandwiches they were taking with them.

The trio was ready for their adventure.

"I want you two to know I'm plotting my revenge," Ciara said as they packed her trunk with gear to survive twelve or more hours in the elements. Despite the recent snow, the sidewalks had been shoveled. "I am so mad at both of you for getting Daddy all worked up."

"I'll be forgiven if you two get married." Amber gave her an angelic smile.

"Or not." Ciara squinted. "I haven't dated in months, and now you're trying to marry me off?"

"Yep. Daddy would be proud."

"I agree with Amber, which is scary in itself." Jessica looked dumbfounded. "One, if this guy shows up, then he's interested. I love my husband, but some things he wouldn't do when we dated—shopping with me—was crossed off the list. Two, you gave him your itinerary, so you want him to show up."

"I mentioned it. There's a difference."

Was it? Today was about sisterhood. She rearranged the portable chairs in the trunk to make room for their new pop-up tent and the battery-operated portable generator, which Amber said she'd charged. There was a thrill of being first to grab those bargains. Some deals were so ridiculous that even the bigger stores couldn't offer them.

"Plus, nobody gets in line for these sales unless they're serious shoppers," Ciara added, "and I don't think Sterling is one of us."

"A friendly wager?" Mischief danced in Amber's eyes as she handed Ciara the blankets and then the games they would need to endure the nighttime boredom and temperatures.

"Count me out." Ciara wasn't about to get into that foolishness. "I had a casual conversation with a donor. I'm not sure if he gave it a second thought and will show up."

"*Hmmm.*" Jessica wrinkled her forehead. "Why did you pack an extra chair?"

"In case one breaks." Ciara shrugged. "Come on. Will you get in so we can go?"

"The way you were smiling back in the kitchen, you looked like it was a done deal that he would meet you there," Jessica said.

If he comes, Ciara thought.

The drive to Accent Electronics was brief thanks to light holiday traffic.

When Ciara pulled into the plaza, a dozen customers had already claimed their spots in line.

"Wow, and I thought we were early." Jessica jumped out at the curb, and Ciara popped open the trunk. "I'll grab the generator and tent for when the temperature drops"—another must-have for the stakeouts— "which might be sooner than later. Park, and you and Amber get the rest."

Minutes later, with their stakeout arsenal in tow, Ciara and Amber headed for Jessica.

Once the sisters had claimed their spot and set up their oversized camping chairs, they greeted familiar faces in line. The best defense against assault was knowing your neighbor and looking them in the eyes. Daddy Summers' Lesson 101. They recognized familiar faces from previous years that came for the thrill.

Bundled like sports fans in the frozen rotunda of the Packers Stadium in Green Bay, Wisconsin, they sipped on hot chocolate as the winds picked up.

"What's on your shopping list?" Amber said.

"Video games, headphones, cell phones. I saw an air fryer on sale and other goodies. If there are any flat screens left, I might grab one or two." Ciara called off the items as she mentally counted the cash on hand to stay within her Christmas budget. These gifts were for her family cases who didn't make Help 100 Families list. There were also others on the list who had received low donations, although donations did come in a few months after the new year.

"That's an ambitious list."

The voice. His voice. Ciara's breathing and heart were out of sync. She glanced over her shoulder and came face-to-face with the handsome man who caused her to shiver as if her skin was exposed to the elements.

"Sterling."

He wore a skullcap with a plaid scarf and a jacket that she doubted would keep him warm.

"I told you I would come," he said, as if she did indeed invite him. The power of suggestion.

"Hello, ladies. Thanks for letting me crash your... what did you call it? A stakeout." He grinned.

Amber gave Ciara a what-did-I-tell-you look. "My sister packed an extra chair just for you. I'll get it." She made a beeline for the car.

Traitor. Ciara tracked Amber as if she was a moving target, then faced Sterling again as he squatted next to her.

"Since you expected me, I'm glad I didn't disappoint."

The air around them seemed warm. Ciara was speechless as his stare locked with hers.

"Hi. I'm Jessica, the oldest and wisest sister." Sterling shook her hand.

"We granted you permission. We can't wait to get to know you." Jessica gave up her seat, scooted it closer to Sterling, then winked at Ciara.

Her sisters weren't helping. Ciara got to her feet. "Oh, I'm sorry for not introducing them. Here comes Amber, the troublemaker of the family." She squinted.

Sterling made himself as comfortable as he could in the portable chair next to Ciara. "I doubt any of you ladies could be troublemakers."

"Watch, you'll see," Ciara mumbled, then smiled at Sterling. She was still blown away at his presence. "Would you like a blanket and a cup of hot chocolate?"

"Yes, please."

As he sipped on the brew, Sterling seemed content to listen to Ciara and her sisters talk about how much they enjoyed waiting for the holidays sales.

Every now and then, laughter would break out from revelers in the tailgate party atmosphere.

Soon, Amber plugged her ears with earphones while Jessica FaceTimed with her children about what they wanted for Christmas.

"I can't get enough of Christmas. I thought I would grow out of it, but I never have. The family gatherings, gifts, foods and, of course, the reason for the season," Sterling said out of nowhere.

"I love Christmas too." She pointed to the stores in the shopping strip. Their decorations had jumpstarted the holidays even though they weren't open for business. "Red ribbons, and green garland with white lights are understated, but perfect. People overkill it. Simple is the best."

"Noted. Tell me more about your traditions." He angled his body as one leg rested over his knee.

Rugged.

Relaxed.

And dare she say, romantic.

Ciara cleared her throat and focused on his ankle boots. They looked warm.

"Hold up." Jessica wedged a divide between them, motioning a time-out with her hands. "Here's your first test. Can you put up a tent? It's suddenly starting to get cold." She grinned.

Some revelers set up their tents upon arrival, while other shopping enthusiasts waited until dusk, like the Summers sisters.

"Without directions." Amber smirked and removed the headset as if they were only for show.

"Can't promise that." Sterling stood and rested his blanket over Ciara's lap, accepting the tent, which was still in its new packaging.

The ladies watched as Sterling opened the box, reviewed the directions in what seemed like thirty seconds or less, then put it together—right—the first time.

Larry Summers would be impressed.

"Ladies, your castle awaits." He opened the flap and bowed for them to enter.

Ciara giggled. She was attracted to his sense of humor. Inside, she and her sisters covered the ground with painter's plastic, then layered it with their comforters and blankets. Next came the chairs. Soon, all four of them were inside.

Jessica turned on one of two portable generators. As she pulled out a deck of cards for a round of Uno, someone tapped on the tent.

Mandy, a fellow thrill seeker shopper, poked his head inside when Jessica unzipped it. "You ladies alright?" He removed his trifocal glasses and squinted at the newcomer. "I know these sisters, but who are you?"

"Sterling Price. Nice to meet you." Sterling extended his hand in vain.

"I'm watching you. Girls, if you get uncomfortable with this one here, blow the whistle, and all of us will come with our bats."

Mandy slipped on his glasses and took a few steps forward, then double backed.

"If you're not scared, you should be." Mandy added, "Oh, and if I were you, I would leave this unzipped so we all can check on Larry's girls. I would hate to have to use a knife to slice it open and cut you a couple of times—by accident, of course."

"Of course. Understood." Sterling nodded as Mandy walked away. Folding his arms over his knees, Ciara's guest shook his head.

"Ladies, I'm really sorry I intruded. I don't want my presence to make any of you uncomfortable."

As he was about to stand to leave, Jessica ordered him to stay. "We have questions. We want answers."

Sterling seemed pleased. Ciara groaned inwardly. She was about to be embarrassed.

"What's your full name?" Amber took the lead.

"Sterling Hamilton Price."

"Age, sex at birth, ethnicity?" Amber continued.

"Thirty-six, male, eighty-one percent Sub-Saharan African, sixteen-point-eight percent European, and two-point-two percent East Asian and Native American."

Ciara smirked. This man needed no rescue.

"Smart aleck. *Hmmmph*." Amber lifted a brow. "Okay. I can play that game. What's your credit score, criminal history—"

"Amber!" Ciara frowned at her sister.

"It's okay, as long as she doesn't ask for my social security number. My credit score is seven-ninety-two, and I have no criminal past or juvenile record."

Sorry, Ciara mouthed.

"It's okay. I asked for this."

No, you didn't, Ciara thought.

"That was Amber's warmup. Let's talk about marriages, divorces, child custody, paternity." Jessica folded her arms. "Go."

"I haven't been married—yet." Sterling's glance at Ciara was so brief that if she had blinked, she would have missed it. "I have no children but hope to be a father one day."

Jessica exchanged a look with Ciara. "He's got the right scripts. I like him."

Sterling grinned. "Thanks."

Was her older sister done with her interrogation? The mischievous glint in Amber's eyes was a prelude that her baby sister had more. "Tell us about your worst relationship."

Enough was enough. Ciara fumed as she shuddered. "Sterling, you don't have to answer that."

Amber sighed. "This was just getting good. One more question."

Ciara prayed she wouldn't snap. Was her sister about to cross a line?

"How about I tell you what I consider a perfect relationship." Sterling waited for everyone to agree. "Ciara, the reason I'm here on Thanksgiving evening instead of at home with my dad watching the football games is because I want to get to know you outside of a work lunch. Do we enjoy the same things, believe in the same things, do the same things? So far, our shared path is our parents are still living, we have two sisters, and we like to help others, but what else makes you genuinely Ciara Summers?" He chuckled. "Amber would have a kindred spirit with my sister Briana."

Sterling's words held so much passion that it seemed like they were the only ones in the tent.

"Oh, you really want to know?" Ciara fumbled with her winter cap to hide her nervous fingers.

"This isn't a quiz. I'm in no rush. Take your time answering." He cleared his throat and looked between Amber and Jessica. "It could be tonight, tomorrow, this weekend, next week, but I want to know."

His words wrapped Ciara in a cocoon. They didn't need the generator anymore.

"Sounds like a series of dates to me." Jessica stood and yanked Amber up. "I think we need some fresh air."

"No, I don't. I want to hear what Ciara has to say." Amber frowned, but followed Jessica outside, leaving the flap unzipped.

Ciara laughed. "Sorry you walked into their trap."

"I'm not."

During her sisters' absence, Sterling revealed why he came into the office. She had piqued his interest after the phone call so much that he checked her out on the website. "I felt a kindred spirit and hoped you did too."

Ciara opened her mouth, but no words came out. She rubbed her legs while she gathered her thoughts. "I'm flattered by your attraction, wowed by your generosity, and drawn to your honesty. My only hesitation is it's against company policy to direct donors to give to certain cases."

"Which you haven't."

"I know. The families speak for themselves." She wanted to ask whether he upped the amount of his contributions after they met because of her but didn't.

"My donations," Sterling said, patting his chest, "come from the heart, and they will continue."

"Speaking of your heart, you mentioned God at lunch. Talk about your salvation walk."

Here comes the deal breaker. Ciara held her breath. She had read in the third chapter of James around verse ten that out of the same mouth comes praises and curses, and she wanted to know if his Christian walk was limited to Sundays only.

Sterling's stare was intense. "So many of my life experiences have led me to Christ. I told you about the homeless guy. I wanted salvation, and the Book of Acts led me through the process. I repented, the minister baptized me in the name of Jesus, and God filled me with His Holy Spirit. I felt God's power and heard His heavenly language come from my own mouth. I believe the Bible when it says, without holiness no man shall see God. I know I have my flaws, but I thank God for daily repentance as I desire to grow in Him."

"I've had the same experience." Ciara's heart fluttered in adoration. Had God given her an early Christmas gift?

"I'm glad we're in sync."

She sucked in her breath, imagining they were about to share a kiss. Ciara blinked. Where did that thought come from? Where was Mandy to chaperone? The only icebreaker she could come up with was grabbing a deck of cards.

"Those are good answers." She stood. "Now, I think I need some air."

Chapter Four

Sterling thought the games were over when Ciara and her sisters returned minutes later. Nope. Next came the board games. Video games. More card games. He had forfeited bonding with his father over football for this. Plus, he wasn't winning.

All this brain power was making him sleepy and hungry. Why didn't he pack leftovers? Sterling preferred movement versus being stationary in the cold. Hot chocolate and the hearty sandwiches the ladies brought did nothing to keep his feet from going numb.

"You gave us your ancestry, but let's see how Black you are." Jessica smiled.

More games? Sterling trapped a groan. "I supplied my ethnic breakdown."

He looked between the sisters, then returned his gaze to Ciara and lingered on what he saw. When the woman blushed, she twisted him up inside.

"That's only skin deep." Amber grinned. "Black Card Revoked is fun."

A loss in this culture card game would be an embarrassment to his parents, frat brothers, and employees. In college, some of them were known as the trivia titans.

"Bring it on." He puffed out his chest at the same time his hands became cold, even in the gloves. Sterling rubbed them together.

Ciara slipped the gloves off his hands. Her touch accelerated his heart rate. When her soft hands covered his and rubbed them, Sterling thought he'd stopped breathing. "Mittens work best."

Her pampering and sultry voice made this an evening to remember. If their tent was glass, it would be steamed up now. Wow.

Someone nearby churned out Christmas music, and soon, there was a sing-along as Amber gave each player a set of response cards, and then shuffled the deck question cards.

The moment was snatched away, but Sterling was determined to get it back, even if it took all weekend.

As the host, Amber asked the first question. "In *A Different World*, what city was Whitley Gilbert from?"

What kind of question was that? Sterling had seen every rerun, more than once, yet he couldn't remember. "Do I get a hint?"

"Nope." Amber folded her arms, which were stuffed in a thick coat.

"Okay. Atlanta." When Amber shook her head, Sterling kept guessing. "Savannah, Nashville, Miami, Mobile..." He was all over the place.

"Hold up. If you're going to guess, you might as well do it in alphabetical order."

He eyed Jessica. Was her question in jest, or was she serious? "If I have to."

"Stop the torture. Richmond," Ciara guessed and won.

It didn't take long for Sterling to lose his ten points to be knocked out of the game. So much for brotherhood representation. Would Dray and his other frat brothers know this stuff?

Somehow, he stayed awake as time hovered over one in the morning. This was worse than pulling all-nighters studying for college exams, but then again, he was in close quarters with Ciara. She was fun, witty, and beautiful.

The best part: Ciara was a practicing Christian.

"Sterling, you have my stamp of approval." Jessica smiled.

"You seem trustworthy... and genuine, so we're leaving her in your hands. Don't mess this up." Amber gave him a warning with the lift of her brow.

Ciara seemed just as surprised as him when the two sisters packed up their things. "Huh?" An unreadable expression crossed her face. "You're leaving? The store opens in less than three hours. This is what we do together." Ciara's slight pout made him feel terrible.

"Ladies, you don't have to leave. I'll go. A warm bed sounds tempting." Sterling wasn't joking, even if he was wearing thermals, he had purchased from one of his vendors. He had gotten what he came for—to see if his attraction to Ciara was real and if it was mutual. Done.

"I'm sure you meant alone in the bed, but you're not getting out of this. You were brave enough to show up, so now you've got to stick it out." Jessica laughed, and within minutes they were gone.

Had he really messed up their tradition?

Ciara didn't look happy. "I can't believe they left me."

Sterling was dumbfounded on how to respond. He waited to take her cue. Was she suddenly uncomfortable with him?

Angry?

"I guess you've cut the Summers sisters' strings." She shifted to anchor her back against a pile of blankets. "I'm glad you're here. For you to spend part—well, most—of your Thanksgiving with me like this," she said, waving her arm around inside the tent, "means something. You're an amazing man, Mr. Price."

"And cold." He shivered.

She laughed. He was serious. "We have thermal socks and blankets to stay warm."

They wrapped themselves like two burritos. She downloaded a mystery audiobook, and surprisingly, Sterling didn't doze once while they listened. When someone was about to get murdered, the door to the tent opened.

He and Ciara jumped.

"Daddy?"

"M–Mr. Summers?" Sterling stuttered.

The man crawled inside and seemed to consume more space than her two sisters.

"What are you doing here?"

"Protecting you." He frowned at Sterling. "Your sisters called saying they were leaving since this Sterling dude was here. Amber said you didn't have a record. I want to keep it that way—for both of us."

"They set me up." Ciara twisted her lips. "I thought they were bluffing or visiting others in line since I drove."

"They took an Uber to the house. They should have called, and I would have picked them up." He squinted at Sterling.

Sterling withheld his groan. *Note to self: Beware of Amber who appeared to be a prankster like his younger sister Briana. Not to be trusted with matchmaking.* The night seemed to drag as Mr. Summers asked his own set of questions, including Sterling's weight, height, and how much he could bench press.

"I gotcha by twenty pounds, and I know how to manipulate my muscles in case of attempted assault."

"Yes, sir." *What did I get myself into?*

While Ciara had the nerve to doze, Mr. Summers was an animated talker who showed no sign of weariness. And he also didn't like to be interrupted, so Sterling listened and dared not yawn.

Five a.m. couldn't come soon enough for early birders. Sterling held his bladder a little longer.

There was movement. Sterling felt drugged as he stretched. He peeped out and was surprised to see a line wrapped around the building. They packed up and moved toward the entrance. Once shoppers cleared doors, they raced to their must-have items. Ciara was no exception. To his surprise, he and Mr. Summers made a beeline to the men's room.

This, by far, had to be the worse first date ever.

Chapter Five

Ciara purchased everything on her shopping list and then some. No surprise there. The surprise was she ran out of cash at the checkout.

"Need help?"

Was Sterling's offer only to make a good impression under her father's watchful eyes. Either way, her predicament was embarrassing.

To her shame, Ciara did what she coaxed herself not to do: whipped out her credit card. So, what if she was more than a hundred dollars over budget.

What was the purpose of having credit cards if she couldn't use them? But there would be consequences. "Thanks. I got this." She finished her transaction, and they walked out to the parking lot.

"I'm assuming you're done with your Christmas shopping with this one trip," Sterling said, guiding one of her carts.

Her father trailed as Ciara led the way. He barked and answered for her. "My little princess is just getting started."

"He's right." Ciara smiled while Sterling blew cold air from his mouth as if he had taken a long drag off a cigarette. She had redeemed her points on her charge cards for store gift cards.

Once everything was stuffed inside her trunk and backseat, she hugged and kissed her father goodbye. "Thanks, Daddy. Now go home and get some sleep."

Larry Summers yawned. "Good night, princess. Sterling." He nodded and strolled back to his car.

Ciara turned to Sterling. Where shopping had revitalized Ciara, the man's weariness cracked through his handsomeness. She suspected he couldn't wait for her to release him too. "How did you like the stakeout? Fun, huh?"

"*Hmmm.* No. I've never seen anyone shop like that before. It's like you had the roadmap to the store." His bloodshot eyes brightened and shone with amusement.

Ciara blushed. "It's not called a stakeout for nothing. I cased the store setup a couple of days earlier after work. I have two more places to hit."

"Today?" His jaw dropped.

"Yep. I can get in and out within ninety minutes, then go home." Ciara grinned. She prided herself on efficiency.

"But you don't have any money," she thought she heard Sterling mumble, but he didn't repeat himself. "I like the stakeouts in the movies where I can sit inside a warm car, sipping on coffee and watching a house or criminal through binoculars, but I wouldn't trade our overnight adventure. It gave me a chance to get to know you, your sisters and your father..."

Folding her arms, she leaned on her car. "My father? Did you now? You can tell me the truth."

Sterling glanced away before meeting her eyes again. "I shouldn't have intruded on your time with your sisters—my guilt is real. There's not enough thermal clothes or discounts to make me *ever* want to do this again. Plus," he said, pausing, "I didn't like seeing you go over at the register."

She had heard him right. How embarrassing? "No worries. I know how to balance my budget."

"If you say so." He didn't sound as if she had convinced him.

Sterling stuffed his hands in his pockets and studied her. "I've laid all my cards on the blanket—pun intended." They chucked. "Listen, Ciara, this is an extended holiday weekend. I would like to see you again. The lady's choice, as long as it's not another stakeout."

Twisting her lips in thought, Ciara didn't respond right away.

"Tell me what's your hesitation."

"I want to say yes," she said, smiling, "but you're a donor to our program. I can't jeopardize the families who are depending on your contributions. I'm the face of Help 100 Families. If I say the wrong thing to upset you, you could walk away with the money in your pocket."

"Not happening. I can separate my personal life from business." He stepped closer. "I like what I see. Ciara, it's Christmastime, let's get to know each other. I won't stop giving. Does that make you feel better?"

Ciara looked into his eyes and drowned in his sincerity. "Actually, it does." Relief on his face matched what she was feeling. "Do you skate?"

A lopsided grin spread across his face. "I've got skills. Give me six hours to thaw out, beautiful, and I'll show you my moves. Should have bought me an electric blanket." Sterling gritted his teeth as if he was serious.

"I can add that to my shopping list."

He grabbed her hands and cupped them. "Don't you spend a dime on me, not a penny."

She pouted.

He leaned closer as if he was about to kiss her. *Hmmm.* That would be nice. "Not if you have to charge it."

Money was an oxymoron to this man. Hold it tight or freely give. Sterling had no idea Ciara had a plan B for her money woes.

"It's been a while, but I think I know where my roller skates are." He looked hyped.

"No, not roller skating. Ice skating at Kiener Plaza. You still want to go?"

His hesitancy lasted a moment, then he agreed.

"Great. Meet me downtown around four. It's the annual kickoff to the holiday season. Sweet dreams." She tapped him on the chest, then slid behind the wheel of her car.

Their attraction was strong. They were in sync. This was a perfect backdrop for a sweet holiday romance.

IF THE LOVE OF MONEY is the root of evil, surely shopping has to be a flaw. Sterling didn't want to overthink Ciara's spending habits.

Christmas was supposed to bring out the best in people. Sterling saw the worst, because of peer pressure to buy from commercial ads.

To keep up with appearances with her friends, his sister Danielle, who lived out of town, flirted with a gambling addiction. It almost ruined her in college. Sterling came to her rescue without their parents knowing. Since then, Sterling was her accountability partner.

His past girlfriends weren't addicted to casinos, but to men who smelled and looked of money. Their sole purpose was collecting expensive gifts and dinners. A few had collected his emotions and wounded his ego.

More life lessons that drove him to seek God's wisdom in business dealings and relationships.

Ciara. *Lord, please let her be different, besides enjoying the frigid cold like a polar bear.*

He conjured up another scenario for a date besides ice skating. A candlelit dinner in front of a fireplace with no chance of her father popping in.

Thoughts of Ciara kept him company until he arrived at his house. The first task was to crank up the heat to seventy-nine before he rested his keys on the counter.

He undressed but left his thermals on and crawled under the covers. Closing his eyes, Sterling sank into the mattress.

An annoying high pitch caused him to jerk forward. What was that sound? "Where am I?" Was it his smoke alarm? He blinked. Then it registered that it was his father calling. "Note to self: Change Dad's ringtone." Sterling had only been asleep a few hours. "Hello."

"So how was your hot date in the cold?" His father didn't attempt to stifle his laugh.

"Frigid." The word caused his teeth to chatter while sending shivers throughout his body. Should have checked for frostbite. "I met her sisters and father."

"Interesting... and on the first date." He paused, then repeated whatever Sterling's mom said near him. "Do you plan to see her again? She'd better be hot stuff for you to leave your old man hanging to watch the games."

"Thomas Price, I watched those games with you to keep you from sulking," he heard his mother fuss.

"Hush, woman," his father replied.

It was Sterling's turn to chuckle. At thirty-six, he wanted that blend of love and laughter in a marriage. "Yes, Dad. Today at four, which is why I'm trying to recover. We're going skating." Sterling hid his groan.

"That's high energy. At least you know she believes in staying fit," his father said.

"And it's inside," his mother added.

"I wish. We're going to Kiener Plaza Downtown. *Ugh* I'm trying to get as much heat in my bones for as long as I can." Closing his eyes, he fell back in bed to the sound of his parents' roar before they ended the call. Why hadn't he thought to ask her ice or roller skating before committing? Why hadn't he asked for her number in case he decided to cancel? Too many questions. Snuggling into his pillow, he drifted off without answers.

Too soon, his alarm woke him. Sterling never craved sleep as much as he did at this moment. He rolled over, thinking. Sterling prayed for the right relationship to complete him. Was Ciara special enough to answer his prayers?

He threw the covers back and headed to the bathroom. When Sterling stepped out of the shower, he had renewed energy to see Ciara again. The *Star Wars* ringtone played as he slipped a black turtleneck on top of a clean thermal T-shirt.

"What's up, man?" Dray said when Sterling answered. He was on the road, hunting for more Black businesses that needed help.

"I'm getting ready to meet Ciara at the ice-skating rink." Sterling braced his ego for his friend's ribbing. He counted the seconds before Dray whooped.

"You survived a night at the North Pole, and you're going back for more? Good luck." His friend continued laughing. "What's the compatibility again? It's got to be more than looks. You can get that anywhere."

"There's this alluring sweetness about her... I'm still feeling her out. Can't learn everything after one date." *With chaperones*, he kept to himself.

"I'm hearing the 'but' you aren't telling me. Whatever. My advice is to walk away now," Dray said. "Don't get blinded by a pretty face."

Sterling nodded. "She's more than that. Ciara's passionate about others. I mean, she works at a nonprofit to help families. I met her through Help 100 Families campaign—"

"Okay, what's the 'but' about her? Bad breath. Bad hair? Bad attitude? I'm trying to be nice here."

"None of that. Ciara's gorgeous. It's just that the way that woman spent money. Had me wondering if we're a good fit. I mean, I'm all for Christmas cheer, but not going for bust."

"*Hmmm.* You've got to watch out for materialistic chicks. That's why you and I aren't married today. Keep your wallet on lockdown."

No way Sterling would mention he had offered to help Ciara with the shortage.

"I still can't believe you agreed to another outdoor event. It's feeling like December in November. You hate wintry weather."

Sterling rubbed his forehead. "I can tolerate thirty and under while getting in and out of my car or house. Anything else, I'd rather hibernate with the groundhog."

"I toast you with my Jack Daniels to a memorable Disney on Ice. See you next week." Dray ended the call.

"I've got to get him in church before Jack Daniels destroys Dray's kidneys." Despite his friend's bad drinking habits, he was the mouthpiece of their business. He had chosen to go out of town to meet with potential clients who would open new markets for Every Dime We Spend.

Sterling finished dressing, grabbed his jacket, cap, and gloves, then headed to his destination.

Ciara was dancing in place to stay warm, looking around for him when he drove up and parked at the meter on Market Street. Good. Proof she wasn't a cold climate–loving reindeer.

Waving, she smiled, and Sterling forgot about the record-low November temperatures that reminded him of December.

"Hi." Her eyes sparkled with excitement. The minty scent from her breath seemed to kiss his lips. "Ready?"

She led the way without waiting for his response. To Sterling's surprise, what he wore did shield him against the wind. After a few awkward slips, they skated in harmony. Sterling couldn't believe how his roller-skating skills transferred smoothly on ice if they didn't move too fast or attempt Olympian spins.

With their arms gripped around each other's waists, he teased her about their "first date."

"Is it okay for me to ask you something about Help 100 Families program?"

"Depends on the question."

Feeling more confident, Sterling twirled Ciara under his arm.

"What are some of the cases that don't make the list?" Sterling asked, and he could feel her body stiffen as she began to slip. He caught her with little effort.

She faced him. "I'm not at liberty to discuss the specifics of cases." She squeezed him closer when small children ran circles around them. "When it comes to my profession, I'm not a rule breaker. When I told you no to lunch the first time, I thought it wouldn't look good to mix business with personal relationships, but my sisters convinced me lunch or getting to know you was harmless."

"I knew there was a reason why Jessica and Amber are my favorite people. Just curious. I hope my dollars are making a difference."

"Yes, professionally and personally." Ciara laughed. "We would have never met if you hadn't donated in the first place. To be honest, I needed Jessica and Amber to reason with me because I wouldn't have gone out with you otherwise. The best way not to do that and keep my job is to leave 100 Hep Families out of the conversation."

"Noted and respected." He smiled to himself. Ciara was the reason he had upped his donation amounts without going over his allocation for charity. "I hope you have no regrets going out with me."

"No, I don't." Her eyes sparkled. "You're like an early Christmas gift."

"I like that." Sterling grinned and puffed out his chest. "I'm careful about getting into relationships too—no drama, no lies. It's something about this time of year that makes me want to experience the holidays with someone special. It's important to me that we share Jesus is the only reason for this season. Our family doesn't do Santa anything."

"That's why I moved you up a notch. We don't either, plus we limit our gift giving."

Huh? What Sterling witnessed back in the store was no limits. He didn't point that out as he pushed one of her carts of loot. Her trunk seemed ready to swallow them up with secret compartments hidden to the naked eye.

Don't make a judgment call. Everything within you knows she's different. Get to know her.

The ex-girlfriends wouldn't have hesitated to take his money at the register for their purchases. "When's the last time you attended a Christmas party?"

She held on tighter as they rounded the rink. "We have them every year in the office. We exchange gifts, bring in potluck and dress in festive colors and ugly sweaters. That's about it."

Sterling chuckled. "Every Dime We Spend is a tad bit more upscale. We're hosting our annual Christmas party in two weeks on December 10th at the Moonrise Hotel. I would like for you to be my guest."

Ciara seemed to give it some thought, then sped up. "*Oooh.* I get to dress up. Yes." Ciara's eyes danced in excitement. "Thank you for asking me."

"It's a small party for our thirteen employees and their spouses or significant others. Also, since you like the cold, I would like to challenge you to a snowball fight after the next snowfall. Gather your sisters and your dad too. You'll lose against my family."

Ciara stopped and patted her chest, almost causing a collision. "What? You do winter activities?"

He kept her steady. "Hey, I told you I like all seasons. I'm not a fan of staying outside for hours when I can be inside a warm house or car."

"You are so going to get a beat down. My folks are relentless." She laughed. "Sterling, this is exciting. I'm really glad we're getting a chance to know each other." They rounded the curve with ease.

"Me too. Hot chocolate?"

"Yes, please."

"Let me guess: You want to drink it outside."

"Nah. I'm cold."

"Shocking." The woman was full of surprises. Sterling laughed as they slid off the rink at the exit. After returning their skates, the pair strolled inside a nearby restaurant for refreshments.

Ciara claimed a table while he ordered at the counter. Although they were inside, both kept on their jackets.

While he sipped from his cup, Sterling admired her beauty. "How about attending church with me on Sunday and make it three days in a row getting to know me?"

Tilting her head, she didn't hide her adoration. "Sterling Price, you're showing me how truly special you are. You've beat me from asking you."

"Is that yes?"

"It's an of course."

Chapter Six

"So," Jessica said, smacking her lips over the phone, "another date? Daddy didn't scare off Mr. Handsome, and we know he tried."

A smile crept across Ciara's face as she applied a hint of shimmer. "This is the first man ever to invite me to his church. That alone is a recipe for falling in love, girl." Tilting her head, she thought about it. "Well, maybe not, but I guess he's backing up his 'I live to impress God' statement."

"I'm impressed. Usually, it's the woman trying to corral the man through the church door, then applying Krazy Glue on the seat to keep him from escaping before God calls him out."

"See, aren't you glad Amber and I told you to take a chance?" Jessica didn't mask her told-you-so tone.

"For the second or third time, yes. He's exciting. Nice. Handsome, and has a job. Yesterday or early this morning, Sterling took me to a midnight bowl. I didn't know I could bowl." She grinned at the memory. The atmosphere was casual and energetic.

"Since when? How many strikes did you get?" Jessica quizzed her.

Ciara jutted her chin at her reflection in her bathroom mirror. "Two."

Jessica laughed. "Two more than the last time we went. When was that, a year ago? You still can't bowl, but I'm sure Sterling will teach you."

"I don't know when I'm going to be available. Considering I'm job hunting for something part-time to finish my holiday shopping, but I'm glad we were able to pack in so many dates in a short time." Ciara shivered with excitement.

Jessica sighed. "You overspent on the first day again?" She sounded disappointed. "And I know you're not finished with your charity spending."

"Yeah, I did and no, I'm not." Ciara wasn't happy about that either, but more people came to mind when she saw certain items. "But some good news: I paid off my car as I planned. Six months ahead of schedule."

"Again. That's so you." Jessica chuckled. "Unbalanced spending. You run a tight ship for yourself, but when it comes to others this time of year, you lose focus."

"It's better to give than receive," Ciara said in reverence of God's Word in Acts 20:35. "Sis, as a mechanical engineer, you don't see what I see. One act of kindness can go a long way. If I get on at a retail store, like I did a few years back, I can use my employee discount for other stuff."

"I hate when you get yourself in this bind, but it's you being you. What is Mr. Price going to say about your non-availability?"

Ciara flipped the off switch as she walked out of her bathroom. "He doesn't pay my bills or have a ring on my finger."

"Just make time for him. Sterling seems like a good guy."

"He is, and he invited me to his company Christmas party."

"See. Another invite—" Justin Junior's yell was heard in Jessica's background. "Girl, let me get my children ready. I guess they don't know how to ask their father."

"Bye." Ciara appraised her outfit, a gold turtleneck sweater dress, brown knee-high boots, and a festive scarf around her neck. She was feeling giddy, thinking about seeing Sterling again. Ciara grabbed her Bible on her way out the door.

She knew she'd reached her destination when the House of Blessings came into view from the highway. It was a large complex with a small parking lot, judging by the traffic jam. When she cleared the entrance, Ciara snagged the first vacant spot, then bundled her cape as she strolled to the glass double doors where red metallic bows decorated twin oversized wreaths. She spied Sterling speaking with a couple, but he stopped when he saw her walk inside.

He quickened his steps, and without warning, he engulfed her in a hug. That gesture startled her at first, even though hugging was part of their church culture.

Sterling's embrace felt natural and sincere, not mischievous or forced, so Ciara surrendered to the greeting. She would no longer fight this emotion.

Although she hadn't been on the lookout for a relationship, a relationship found her, and it had been accelerating for weeks now. Her father's rendition of Donny Hathaway's "This Christmas" played in her head.

"Welcome." Sterling looked into her eyes as if he was noting her features for the first time. He stepped away from their hug and led the way into the sanctuary.

As customary in her church, she knelt at her pew to give thanks for being in God's presence again. He joined her on bended knee.

They faced each other with smiles as they took their seats as the musicians struck the first chord of an upbeat Christmas song.

At the end of the selections, Sterling's pastor approached the podium in the pulpit. He welcomed guests, made announcements, then Pastor Franklin opened his Bible.

"I'll call my sermon 'There's No Magic in Christmas.' God's blessings are real, and Jesus' mercy is renewed every morning, not just one day of the year." He paused to glance at his notes.

"The Lord is calling us not to follow after the glitz and overindulgence of this world, whether it's food or shopping. It's a trap. The best gift is to love one another and extend kindness. Invest in relationships, in each other's souls..."

Ciara sat on the edge of her seat, soaking up the message. She appreciated sermons that didn't sugarcoat the Scriptures. "Yes."

Sterling leaned closer and whispered, "I'm guessing you're connecting with my pastor." He smiled. "I'm glad."

She nodded, so as not to break her focus. Before Ciara realized it, Pastor Franklin had ended his sermon. The altar call followed with souls responding to the invitation for prayer and the water baptism in Jesus' name once they repented.

When the pastor announced it was offering time, the congregation applauded. Ciara loved their spirit of giving. This had to be where Sterling got his inspiration.

She recalled hearing about a woman who put a quarter in an offering because she wanted to give God something, and the Lord later blessed her in an abundant way.

After the benediction, Sterling grabbed her hand and squeezed it.

"Come on. My parents sit on the other side, and I know they want to meet the celebrity."

"Me?" Ciara patted her chest. "How?"

"Getting me to do the stakeout. They couldn't believe it since I enjoy six to eight hours of sleep, and football is the only bribe to get me outside in the cold. And snowball fights." He grinned.

Sterling led her to where a small group had gathered and watched them approach, then applauded Ciara like a superstar. Bystanders turned their heads at the commotion adding to her embarrassment.

"These are my parents, Phyllis and Thomas Price."

Ciara nodded. "It's nice to meet you both."

A mature version of Sterling stepped forward and snickered. "You deserve an award, getting my son out of his comfort zone. I love it."

His mother, an elegant woman with kind eyes, smiled. "It's nice to meet you, dear."

Next, Ciara met Briana, one of his sisters. His family's friendliness made her feel welcome. Sterling pulled her away when they fired one question after another.

"Son, please bring Ciara by soon."

"Okay, Mom." The couple waved goodbye.

"I like them and your church. Thanks for inviting me," Ciara said.

"Thank you for accepting. Brunch?"

"Of course. It's a free meal," she teased, then trailed Sterling in her car to the Peacock Diner in the Loop, blocks from St. Louis city limits. Their booth seat rotated like a carousel. His eyes smiled as he studied her. While indulging in breakfast tacos and pancakes, Ciara felt the unspoken electricity between them.

"Enjoying yourself?" Pure adoration shone in his eyes.

Contentment consumed Ciara. "Yes. I have all weekend."

"I aim to please, Miss Summers. When will you allow me to pick you up from your home and take you on a date, not meet up somewhere?"

Tomorrow, Ciara wanted to say, but the work week meant back to reality. "Next weekend."

"Lunch in between?" Sterling had expectancy in his eyes.

"Maybe." She shrugged with a smile.

They parted ways with a hug and ended the night after a two-hour phone call.

On Cyber Monday, Ciara strolled into the office in high heels and spirits. Christmas had come early for her in the relationship department.

Hours later, her spirit plummeted after she downloaded the weekend donations for the cases profiled in the newspaper. Out of thirty-nine families, three hadn't received anything—yet. One passed over was one too many. These people only had bare necessities. Her heart bled.

Lord, stir up people's hearts to give. Ciara thought about Sterling's generous heart.

She craved to hear his voice. If only she could steer him and so many others toward the families who had been overlooked. Gnawing on her lips, she wondered if she could somehow hint about situations like the ones profiled.

Christians are honorable. Blessed are you whose ways are blameless of wrongdoing, God whispered.

Sterling agreed to separate his giving to the program and their relationship, so why was she struggling and being tempted? And the Lord called her on it. She needed to start an email and phone campaign to solicit donations.

"You're right," Ciara mumbled.

"Who's right?" Terri asked as she walked into Ciara's office.

"God."

"Oh." Terri wore a clueless expression. "Anyway, I'm about to start putting Christmas decorations up in the lobby, so can you listen out for anyone who walks in as I get stuff from the storage area?"

"Sure." Ciara smiled at the receptionist, but her mind was elsewhere. Every year, she faithfully put money aside in a Christmas savings account to assist needy families—if needed. But with new ones profiled each weekend, the earlier cases were soon forgotten by the end of the week.

For the next couple of hours, Ciara worked on crafting emails to solicit funds from local small business to major corporations.

When Ciara took a break, she turned her attention to find seasonal positions online. Hopefully, before the end of the week, she would have that second job to help others and, at the same time, she could wipe out the credit card debt she had incurred.

The next day, Help 100 Families scored big on #GivingTuesday, to Ciara's delight. The global initiative to switch consumers' mindset after going for broke at stores on Black Friday and Cyber Monday online shopping was working. It was as if God steered donors to her forgotten families.

"Thank you, Jesus."

Still, it wasn't enough. She ran the report of past supporters who hadn't made contributions this year. Ciara had no problem calling them.

Wednesday brought good news—sort of. Walmart scheduled her for an interview after work. They were offering a signing bonus. It was on for her to secure the seasonal position.

Ciara left her day job a half hour early to make the interview. When she arrived at Walmart, a shopping frenzy had the parking lot packed. She circled the aisles twice before snagging a spot.

Her phone rang as she trekked across the lot. Sterling. They had taken a selfie at the ice rink, and she'd uploaded the photo to his name and as her screensaver. "Hi."

"Lady, I missed talking to you during the day. Hungry? If you're not busy, want to meet me for dinner?"

Ciara pouted as she kept a steady pace to the entrance so as not to be late. "I can't. I'm heading inside Walmart."

"More shopping?"

"More like more money. I have a job interview." She looked both ways at the crosswalk in front of the doors before proceeding.

Sterling was silent. Too quiet.

Were they still connected? Ciara called his name to make sure. "I'm inside. Let me call you back." She disconnected, headed to the customer service department, and asked for Tanya as the email she'd received had instructed.

After a fifteen-minute wait, a short, plump woman hurried toward her out of breath. "Sorry. Ciara, right?"

"Yes." Ciara nodded and smiled.

"Follow me. Sorry. I had some irons to put out—lazy employees," Tanya ranted, speed walking through the maze of shoppers.

Ciara had to skip a few times to keep up until they reached a small back room in the superstore.

Settled at the table, Ciara caught her breath. Tanya scrutinized her application as if an upper-management position was available instead of a store associate.

As the clock on the wall clicked, Ciara watched the woman's expression as she made up her mind.

"Welcome aboard," Tanya said, nodding. "How soon can you start?"

Ciara did a mental review of her schedule. Before she could answer, Tanya stood, and reached for smock off a hook, then handed it to Ciara. "If you can start now, you'll receive a two-hundred-dollar signing bonus after working thirty days."

This evening? Ciara didn't know the signing bonus meant starting the day of her interview. "Okay," slipped from her mouth before she could trap it. And that was that. Ciara put her things in a locker and slipped on the vest with the Walmart logo.

"Since this is your first shift, I'll only assign you to two areas to keep tidy." Tanya didn't take questions as she walked out of the room, glancing over her shoulder with an expression that Ciara better be behind her.

Keeping the children's clothing and the craft sections in order was not a task meant to be performed in a dress and heels.

The five-hour shift seemed like seven with a too short dinner break to gobble down a Subway sandwich. Why didn't she tell Tanya she would start tomorrow? That way, she could be enjoying dinner with Sterling.

Remnants of the stakeout and ice skating were catching up with her body. Her back ached. This wasn't her first time working a seasonal job during Christmas, but this was the first time she wasn't overjoyed to do it.

Ciara raced out the exit after signing out on the computer. She wasn't far from her house, but she was so tired, she could have climbed in the backseat for a nap. When she got home, Ciara haphazardly went through her nightly regimen before she slid to her knees. "Thank You, Jesus, for this blessing." She yawned. "God, give me strength to last these thirty days..." which would take her into the New Year a week or so, and she guessed, to accept returns. She wasn't looking forward to that either.

Be careful what you ask for, because I gave it to you, God whispered.

The next morning, Ciara dressed in more comfortable clothes for her second shift that she was scheduled to work every day for the rest of the week, except Sunday.

Sterling called her while she was headed to the office. "I missed hearing your voice last night."

"Sorry. I was tired when I got home." She stifled a yawn. "I was hired on the spot."

"Oh." Silence. "Can I ask why you are working a second job?"

Isn't it obvious? Ciara thought. "An extra paycheck."

"If you need money—"

Slowing down at the light, she shook her head. "If you're about to offer, thank you, but I'm not that type of woman to take a man's money."

"But if you need it, I'd rather give it to you than see you work two jobs."

She smiled at his thoughtfulness but declined his help. "I prefer your money go to the families of your choice."

Sterling's sigh came over loud, and clear, as if she had increased the volume. "At the moment, you're my choice. How long do you plan to work this second job?"

"Long enough for me to collect my thirty-day signing bonus." She had twenty-nine days to go.

"Would I be out of line to ask why?"

How should she answer that? She didn't need or want anyone else on her back besides her family about her methods to help families at Christmas. "I'd rather not say right now. Look, I'm here. Can we talk later?"

"I plan to see you later. I'll bring lunch or dinner."

Ciara smiled as they ended the call. She didn't care if Sterling brought her breakfast or a cookie. She craved to see him and soak up his smile whenever he looked at her. "Okay. Bye."

WHAT WAS I THINKING? Sterling held his head in his hands. Had he tried to bribe Ciara? He was clearly overthinking things.

Was that desperation talking? Sterling wondered. She hadn't asked for financial assistance or accepted his offer. This relationship was worth exploring—when she wasn't working.

Since seeing Ciara was on hold for a few hours, he checked in with his father. He felt guilty for skipping out on his family most of the Thanksgiving weekend. "Hey, Pops."

"Oh, you're back from the honeymoon." His father chuckled.

He grunted. "Honeymoon? I don't think so, not after a few dates." There was only frustration trying to get to know Ciara.

"But you do like her. I could see it when you introduced us at church. You two keep spending time together, things will change."

"Too late." Sterling huffed. "She's making me re-think things, and honestly, I don't know if that's a good thing." He frowned and worried his mustache.

"What do you mean, son?" The amusement in his voice was gone.

"I can't figure Ciara out. I like her—I really like her. She's sweet, fun... but spends a lot of money and now she needs to work two jobs." He paused and exhaled for the final blow. "I can't believe I offered to help her to keep her from working so hard. That's not me. Who am I?"

Sterling slapped his forehead and huffed out his self-annoyance.

"You're my son who's kind, smart, and at times, overly suspicious of people when it comes to money." He cleared his throat. "Did she accept?"

"No, she didn't."

"See. Not every woman wants your money. Don't let past misjudgments cloud your current perceptions. Pray and ask for His wisdom."

"You're right." Sterling bobbed his head. "I was wondering if I've been a magnet for bank withdrawals with women. Thanks for the pep talk and reminding me to go to God. I'd better go, so I can work on the December budget."

Thomas chuckled. "I understand. I'm proud of you, son—and Dray. You both have done good. Talk to you later."

Sterling ended the call and did an instant replay of their conversation.

"Hey, no sleeping on the job." His business partner, Dray, tapped on Sterling's open door, then strolled in.

"I wasn't asleep."

"Daydreaming about someone?" Dray grinned and flopped in a chair.

Sterling ignored his friend's digging. "Welcome back. Congrats on sealing the contracts in Kansas City, Nashville, and Memphis—that was a surprise. You, my brother, have been busy."

"Just me doing me." Dray leaned forward for a fist bump. "Memphis was an early Christmas present. The owner of Fred's

Auto Shop has been stringing us along for months. Have you finalized plans for our holiday party and end-year bonuses?"

"I'm playing catch-up." Sterling looked away, guilty of slacking.

"Huh? You told me you would have it done before the Thanksgiving break."

"I've been distracted."

"Ciara?" Dray gave him a side-eye. "I leave you in charge for a week, and you blow it."

That was the running joke between the equal partners whenever one of them traveled. "Hey, man, remember to stay up on your contributions in December. I can't—we can't—let Kenneth win again."

"There are no losers. We all win."

"Whatever, man." Dray crossed an ankle over his knee. "Now, did you take pictures at the shopping stakeout?" He bent over, laughing. "Was this woman worth freezing your behind?"

When Sterling was slow to answer, Dray stopped laughing. "What?"

Twisting his lips, Sterling considered his answer. "She's worth it, but... I know people go overboard with Christmas cheer. She's spending a lot of money, and she now has a part-time job."

"At least she's not spending yours or the company's money."

I offered, though. Sterling kept that remark to himself.

"Talk to her about your concerns." Dray shrugged like it was no big deal.

"Not my place, not after three weeks. You, on the other hand, need to re-think things. Donations are not supposed to put you in debt."

Sterling might not have any say over Ciara's affairs, but as co-owner, he would not allow Dray to bankrupt the company for the sake of winning a bet.

Chapter Seven

Ciara yawned. She had skipped lunch so she could make a stop before heading to her second job. This was day three working a second shift, and she wished it was day thirty.

Her heart was heavy. She couldn't shake the profile of case number thirty-seven.

A twenty-five-year-old single mother with three children is coping with the sickle cell disease. The two family flat where they stay on the first floor caught fire and damaged the kitchen, but with nowhere else to go, they return at night to sleep there. She can't keep a job because of her constant flare-ups. Her needs are many, but bedroom furniture and warm clothes for the children would help her faith in God and people. One toy for each child would warm her heart.

How safe was a house to live in after it caught on fire? Too bad Walmart got rid of its layaway. Otherwise, Ciara could have put some things away for them.

After she left the office, Ciara visited a family in a neighborhood that bordered downtown on Salisbury Street.

Three generations of Greens lived in a house that begged for a makeover—paint being the priority for it as well as a handful of their neighbors. Despite the homeowners' meager possessions, the majority on the block had their yards decked out with decorations that could be featured in a nostalgic Christmas movie.

The Greens had a faded plastic Santa that took center stage among reindeers, elves, angels, and a Black nativity scene. The strings of lights had missing bulbs, but those that had survived over the years twinkled brightly.

She parked and hiked the steep stairs where a handmade wreath reminded her of a child's craft project. Ciara called this unscheduled visit a wellness check for her own peace of mind.

Ciara didn't have to be on the clock to care. The "It's more blessed to give than receive" Scripture rang true more during the Christmas season, whether people knew it was from the Bible or not.

Despite the support of nonprofit agencies, churches and philanthropies, some families fell through the cracks.

She rang the bell and waited to hear Mrs. Green's house slippers shuffle to the door. A curtain swung back and forth before the door opened.

"Miss Summers." The woman smiled. "We didn't expect you, or I'd have made a pot of greens."

"No worries. I wanted to check on my people." That's what Ciara called her cases—her people.

"You're welcome anytime. I do have some fresh-baked apple pi—"

"Miss Summers," little Bryan cheered. He raced toward her barefoot on the yellowing linoleum floor that stretched from the front door to the kitchen.

The thin layer of plastic that covered the inside of the windows hinted of the house's air pockets.

"Boy, didn't I tell you to put on some socks." Mrs. Green frowned at her four-year-old grandson.

Ciara followed her into the sitting area sparsely furnished with thick yellowing and cracked plastic protecting the chairs and sofa. Footprints left marks on the olive-green carpet. The Christmas tree tilted in the corner, displaying more handmade decorations. Five presents were underneath.

More gifts were coming. Ciara had already shopped for them. Her niece and nephew had a ball wrapping gifts for other children.

"I do have dessert." Mrs. Green's plump body wobbled from side to side as she disappeared way down the hall to her kitchen.

Her daughter, Arlene Green, appeared with Shanay anchored on her hip, gripping onto her mother's sweater. Mason and April trailed behind. Her children were stair-steppers: six, five, three and ten months.

"Hey, Ciara," Arlene greeted with annoyance. "Are you bringing us word on any more assistance? Time is counting down and I can't hold on much longer."

Lord, are donations enough to keep Arlene from splitting up her children in the foster care system, or giving up custody altogether for adoption, because she feels hopeless as a parent? Five years younger than Ciara, Arlene was separated from her off-and-on boyfriend, Bryan Sr., the children's father.

"Sorry, no. I stopped by to check on you before the weekend to make sure you didn't need anything." Ciara smiled.

"Aren't you sweet? I got it under control." Mrs. Green stretched the food allowance on her daughter's monthly eWIC card to make sure her grandchildren wouldn't go hungry.

Plus, Ciara didn't want to give the impression that her visits were strictly business. She wanted to see them thrive.

Mrs. Green returned with a slice of apple pie and ice cream.

Ciara never understood how people could enjoy ice cream in the winter. She was a seasonal eater. Ice cream for the summer and chili or hot cocoa for the winter. "Yummy, but I'm going to have to eat fast. I've got a second job during the holidays."

"I wish I could find something from home. I can't afford the childcare, and it's too much for Mom for eight hours."

"Awww, don't you worry about me," the elderly woman hushed her daughter, then smiled at Ciara. "Miss Summers, I'm surprised someone hasn't snatched you up."

Arlene rolled her eyes. The baby on her hip began to fuss. "I have the evidence of being snatched. It ain't all that." She pointed to her children, then left the room.

Sadness covered Mrs. Green's face. "My daughter's broken, but I'm believing the good Lord will put her back together."

"Yes, Jesus can. I'm reminded of that when my services are no longer needed because lives have changed." That wasn't going to happen on this Earth since Jesus had prepared a place for those He saved from their sins. Ciara finished her dessert and readied to leave. "Sorry to cut my visit short, but I have to go."

Mrs. Green walked her to the door. "Have you heard anything about our case?"

"Your story will be highlighted this weekend." Case numbers forty-two to fifty-six would be profiled. The Greens were number fifty-one.

"Lord, send someone with deep pockets." Mrs. Green folded her hands and looked toward heaven.

WITH A HOT MEAL IN tow, Sterling entered Walmart on the hunt for Ciara. He did a quick scan of the registers—nope—then the customer service counter. He continued his mission, next patrolling the aisles for Ciara.

Sterling felt the heat seeping from his package before he found her in the toy department. Either she was positioning or playing with the stuffed animals on the shelves. "Ciara."

She spun around. Her lips curved when she stared into his eyes. That smile made him question why he had questions about their budding relationship. She was special. He felt it at the same time he noticed the weariness in her eyes.

"Sterling, what are you doing here?"

"To see you and to make sure you eat, remember?"

"I forgot, and I'm starved, but my dinner break isn't for another forty-five minutes."

Masking his disappointment that she couldn't take a break, Sterling slipped his hands in his pockets and rocked on his heels. "Then put it up until then."

"Okay." She accepted his bag and sniffed it, then took off, then backtracked a few steps. "Thank you. I'll be right back."

In her absence, Sterling tried to stand clear of the stampede as he watched the madhouse from the sidelines. The aisles were congested. Carts stacked.

Ciara's face glowed when she returned. "Sorry about dinner." She resumed her task.

Without thought, he began to assist her.

She chuckled. "What are you doing?"

"Working." He grinned.

"For free?"

"Assisting you. This is nothing compared to the stakeout." He mimicked what he saw her do earlier with the merchandise.

"That's sweet, but I don't get off until ten-thirty."

"Woman, should I remind you I survived the camping adventure for longer hours?"

She shoved him with her hip and blushed. "You better not get me fired."

"Never." Sterling wiggled a brow. "Would it be a terrible thing if I covered your salary?" He couldn't help himself from offering again. There were so many holiday activities they could explore together.

Clearly, money couldn't buy everything. If this was a test, Ciara won hands down because she didn't take the bait. Right now, he wished she would.

Ciara stopped what she was doing. Her eyes held compassion. "Don't take this the wrong way..." She frowned and seemed to struggle with what to say next. "I can't be bought."

"That's not what I meant." He bowed his head. "I can't explain the Ciara effect you have on me. I want us to spend more time together."

"Forgiven." Ciara blushed, then sobered as she placed her hands on her hips and surveyed the circus activity surrounding them.

A woman popped up from nowhere.

"Ciara," she said, pointing to the mayhem on the floor, "I need you on the register." Tanya, the name badge identified her as the store assistant manager, eyed Sterling from head to toe, then walked away.

"My boss," Ciara mumbled. She stood on her tiptoes and delivered a lingering kiss on his cheek. "I'd better go."

Stunned, Sterling felt like a teenager as he rubbed the side of his face where her touch lingered. "Don't forget to eat," he called after her.

And there it was. Their first kiss. A Friday night. In the toy section at Walmart. Who would forget that?

Chapter Eight

Victory. Ciara had survived four days at Walmart. That's not what her body called it. With all the force she could muster, Ciara rolled over and forced her eyes opened.

"Victory." She moaned and took a deep breath. "For a noble cause," she reminded herself.

At least it was Saturday, and she was scheduled to work a mid-shift, eleven to six. Judging from her short-term experience from the previous nights, she wouldn't clock out on time.

Closing her eyes, Ciara snuggled deeper under her comforters. Then the phone alarm woke her too soon. More alert, she stretched and smiled.

Sterling came to mind. The man had brought her food. When she got a chance to eat it after popping it into the microwave, she enjoyed it more, knowing he had brought it.

Ciara grabbed her phone and tapped his name. "Good morning."

"Morning to you. I'm glad to hear your voice. I missed not talking to you last night, but I guess you were too tired to talk when you got off work."

"Did I dream that you brought me dinner?" she teased as she threw back the covers. "That was so sweet of you. Thank you."

"You're sweet." His chuckle was deep and rich. "Did I dream you kissed me?"

This time, Ciara giggled.

"Sounds like we were in the same dream. In mine I got this passionate kiss—*wow*—from this cute sales associate." They shared the laughter. "Are you working today?"

She glanced out the window before padding her way to the bathroom. "I go in at eleven, and I'm supposed to get off at six, but I'm sure it will be more like seven."

"That's most of the day!"

"Yeah, I know, but I'm off on Sundays. That was the deal." Ciara wasn't budging on that one.

"And next Saturday night for my Christmas party, too, right?"

Had she asked for that day off? Ciara couldn't remember. "*Ahhh,* let me check when I get in."

He was quiet. The gaiety between them dissipated. Ciara would switch shifts if she had to. "Sterling, I'm not going to miss it. I'd better go so I can get ready."

"Want a lift to work? I can be your chauffeur."

"And a handsome driver, too, but I'm good. If you want to visit my church tomorrow, here's an invitation from me. It's God's Apostles Church in University City."

"I know where it is. I'll be there. Maybe we can do brunch afterward. It seems like forever since we've been together."

"I know, and this may sound silly, but I miss you."

"I miss you more."

They ended the call, and Ciara showered, dressed, ate, and backtracked to her bed where she knelt to pray.

How had she been up for an hour and failed to thank God for another day?

She never wanted to forget that. Those who were sick would give anything for another day, hour, even more minutes with loved ones.

Ciara left the house with a sack lunch, in comfortable shoes. Her hair was brushed up into a ball, and she had on light make-up. She was going into a war zone, not a fashion gala.

Tanya had warned Ciara to expect more customers from opening to close until Christmas Eve. She had to circle the parking lot a couple of times to find a vacant spot in the area where associates parked. Countdown to Christmas.

Once she clocked in, Ciara checked next week's schedule and muffled her scream. "Oh, no." Not only wasn't she off, but instead of eleven to six, Ciara was scheduled to work the ten-to-seven shift, which probably would be an eight o'clock sign out. She closed her eyes and rubbed her fist against her forehead. This had to be fixed as soon as she got a chance or find an associate willing to switch their early morning shift with her mid-day hours.

There was little downtime during her shift to speak with Tanya as the woman bounced Ciara from stocking the laundry shelves to relieving on the register. She finished lunch, then was assigned as cashier for the last three hours of her shift.

It was a maze to get to her register. As she counted the cash in her drawer, she spied shoppers in starting position, ready to make the mad dash to her lane. With one flick of the "open" button, her lane resembled an airport security check-in line.

Ciara kept a steady rhythm checking folks out, even when customers changed their minds and she had to take items off one by one until the amount was affordable for the shopper.

She tried not to look at the never-ending stream of carts that blocked aisles and stretched into the clothing departments.

All eyes were on her as if they were willing her to check out faster. Then her skin tingled, which made her look up. Her eyes connected with Sterling's right away. Whenever he looked at her, he was intense with his stare. Everything about him stood out. His smile magnified from where he stood, at least ten customers deep.

His presence recharged her, and Ciara sped through her customers' transaction as if she was being timed as a contestant on a game show.

Her heart pounded as she bagged each shopper's items until Sterling was within reach, two customers away. Ciara did her best not to blush and to concentrate on her tasks. That didn't stop her from blushing.

When it was his turn, he laid two magazines on the conveyor belt.

"Hello..." Sterling leaned closer to read her name tag. "Ciara. What a beautiful name."

She inhaled. For the slightest second, it was just her and him. She exhaled. "Thank you, sir. Is this all for you?"

"No. What I want isn't on the shelves." He snickered and stared at her lips.

"Behave. You could have gone through self-checkout."

"Then I wouldn't be able to see you."

Although he was playful, she sensed Sterling wouldn't play emotional games with her. He said what he felt, and her heart verified it. She lowered her lashes, then chanced another glance at him. "That will be eleven-seventeen. Will that be card or cash?"

"Cash." As if in slow motion, he handed her a twenty. If he stalled any longer, angry customers behind him might revolt.

She gave Sterling his change.

"Text me when you get off. I'll be in my car reading."

"Huh?" Ciara frowned. Had she heard right? "That's not for another hour and a half," she said, then greeted the next person in line.

"I'll be here, waiting for you. All these shoppers aren't out for holiday cheer. Foolishness shows up at night. And if they try something with you, they'll be sorry." In his signature stride, he walked away.

WHAT WAS IT ABOUT CIARA Summers that had Sterling outside in the cold again? At least he was inside his car this time with the heat control at his fingertips.

Sterling stroked his beard, eying customers leaving the store and manhandling their carts to their trunks, reminding him of his shopping experience with Ciara.

He grinned to himself, conjuring up memories of him with Ciara and her father on Black Friday. It was hard to believe that woman who just rang up his magazines was a board member of a nonprofit. There was no air about Ciara—beautiful, kind, passionate, and he was starting to learn, stubborn.

A combination Sterling found fascinating enough for him to sit in his car with two magazines he wouldn't read.

He checked the time. It was five minutes later than the last time. He flipped open the first page as his younger sister's ringtone interrupted him doing nothing. "Hey, Briana."

"Hi, Sterling. What ya doing?"

He chuckled while surveying the parking lot. "You don't want to know."

"*Hmmm.* Now, I think I really do. You and Ciara must be on your way to see *The Nutcracker* since it's opening night at the Fox Theatre."

It was a musical he treated his sister to every year. Shaking his head, Sterling sighed. "I wish. I'm waiting in my vehicle for her to get off her shift at Walmart." Sterling had to turn down the volume on his Bluetooth as his sister cranked up her screams of amusement.

"She gets more interesting every time I talk to you. Definitely not your normal picks."

Sterling grunted. "You mean your picks you set me up with. Ciara's special and different and...unpredictable. You'll like her."

"*Humph.* Sounds complicated to me."

The more Briana tried to end the call, Sterling kept the conversation going. He asked about her social calendar, doctor appointments, and hobbies—anything to keep from reading the magazines.

"I know what you're up to. I love you, but not enough to talk to you until Ciara gets off. Bye." She was gone.

He drummed his fingers on the steering wheel and defaulted to more people-watching. There were other things he could be doing at home, like checking out a sports show or movie, which he could do while he waited, but that would only distract him from watching out for criminal mischief.

A family of four passed by his car. Most of them weren't dressed for the elements with thin clothes and oversized sweaters. Their attire made Sterling shiver. The vehicle they climbed into had several dents. When the car roared to life, his muffler warned pedestrians to lookout as the father drove off. They needed another vehicle. He wondered what other things they might be doing without?

That prompted Sterling to visit 100NeediestCases.org and read over some of the current profiles. After reading a few, Sterling closed his eyes to pray for guidance to bless someone.

Finally, he picked only one and limited the donation to a hundred dollars. His payment was confirmed with a text.

Then he received another one. This time from Ciara.

If you're still in the parking lot, I'm clocking out. See you out front.

He grunted in amusement. **Of course, I'm still here, woman.**

Sterling headed to the entrance. The temperature had dropped, and he left his gloves in the car, so he slipped his hands into his jacket pockets.

When Ciara appeared, her smile brought all the warmth he needed. She looped her arm through his. "Thank you for waiting for me. I'll show you where I parked."

"You're off for next Saturday for the Christmas party, right?"

She stumbled in her steps, but he was there for her rescue. "I'll be there."

They chatted until they reached her car two rows over near the end. This was too far in the dark for her to walk alone, another reason why he didn't like her working this job.

"Thanks for the escort." She unlocked her car.

Sterling opened her door and leaned in for his reward. What was it about sharing kisses at Walmart? "What, no good-night kiss?" he teased, but didn't wait for her response as he brushed his lips against hers—once, then twice. "Good night."

Chapter Nine

"Are your parents here?" Sterling asked as they stood in the foyer of Ciara's church on Sunday morning. His question amused her.

"Yes," she said, laughing, "but I'm not sitting with them this morning. Didn't want to make you nervous."

"How thoughtful, but something tells me Mr. Summers is tracking us with a telescope."

"You have nothing to worry about. Jesus sees what men can't." She patted her chest. "Your heart."

The worship portion was a mix of old and current church melodies. When Pastor Kent walked to the podium, he asked visitors to stand to be acknowledged. Sterling did, along with others, to a hearty applause.

Pastor Kent opened his Bible and read the text for his sermon, Hebrews 12:14: *"Follow peace with all men, and holiness, without which no man shall see the Lord."*

"Peace on earth and goodwill to men is often coined for holiday sermons. I have a twist that is often skipped. Did you read the holiness part?"

Amens and *yeses* floated throughout the audience.

"Ummm-hmmm." Pastor Kent nodded. "Charitable deeds and gift giving isn't a prerequisite for seeing Jesus who sacrificed Himself on the cross. Now, it's our turn by sanctifying our lives under the influence of the Holy Ghost. This Christmas, think

about giving Jesus what He wants from you—a commitment to living a holy life..."

Sterling leaned closer to her ear. "I needed this refresher message that without living holy, I won't see God."

Ciara looked into his eyes and nodded. "I agree."

The sermon must have struck a chord because dozens wanted God's complete salvation package, including the water baptism in Jesus' name and the fire baptism with His Holy Ghost power.

Once the benediction was announced and the offering taken, Ciara gathered her things to get out before her family found them.

Too late.

"Sterling," her father's voice boomed from behind her. Glancing over her shoulder, she spied her family approaching with smiles, including her father who wore the biggest grin.

"Mr. Summers." Sterling extended his hand, and Larry Summers gave him a hearty shake.

"I'm glad to see you here, and you heard the message about holiness." Her father wiggled a brow. "That's what wrong with these young relationships today: They lack purity."

Ciara touched her father's arm. "Daddy, we heard the sermon, and we hid the message in our hearts, so we won't sin against God."

"Glad you can quote it. Live, breathe and meditate on Psalm 119:11." He nodded with an unwavering expression.

"Larry, stop it." Her mother shoved him.

"The Holy Ghost never goes undercover." Sterling's tone was confident, not boastful.

Her father seemed impressed, and Ciara admired him for it. The couple said their goodbyes and headed for the parking lot.

"I can trail you home, so you can leave your car," Sterling said. "Maybe we can visit with my parents."

"Sounds like a plan."

During brunch, Ciara relaxed as they sampled each other's dishes, laughed about unusual holiday traditions, and teased each other about favorite foods. It felt good not to be on anyone's clock.

"Is it me, or do you feel like we've been seeing each other for more than a couple of weeks?" Sterling's eyes twinkled.

"It's not just you." Ciara could feel her vulnerability rising. "I like you being a constant part of my life. Not trying to sound cliché, but you make this season brighter."

He stretched his arms across the table and opened his palms for her to rest her hands. She did. "So, Miss Summers, this has been on my heart: I want us to be exclusive."

Yes! Praise God. Thank You, Jesus. Her heart did a two-step. She blushed. "Thank you for not keeping me waiting and wondering whether that's what you wanted. Ladies don't want to assume. Of course, I want that too."

"Whew. Thank you." Sterling patted his chest. "I didn't want to make assumptions either. I had hoped we could spend a lot of time together. Do you take on second jobs around the holidays all the time?" He frowned, showing wrinkles of concern.

"Nope. Third time." She shrugged and forked a pineapple.

"Oh. Just curious." He picked with his napkin. "What does your father say about this?"

She wanted to ask why he wanted to know, but didn't. "Dad calls me a rebel for a good cause."

"How many more days do you plan to work?" His look was intense.

"After thirty days, I get a two-hundred-dollar bonus." She grinned.

"Thirty days." Sterling frowned and rubbed the back of his head as if it ached. "I've started my stopwatch. Since we're exclusive now, I don't plan to let Walmart come between us."

"Yeah, I've noticed." Ciara grinned and thought about their sweet kisses. She rested her chin in the crook of her hand with her elbows anchored on the table. "Actually, I have twenty-five more days to go."

Soon, they left for the Prices' house, admiring elaborate Christmas decorations along the way. When they arrived at his parents' home, Ciara was treated like an old friend, exchanging hugs with Mrs. Price.

Sterling removed her coat as his younger sister, Briana, gushed over it. "I saw that coat online, but it was sold out before I could order it."

"You have enough clothes to give away." His father chuckled.

"We have hot apple cider, caramel peppermint hot chocolate and Eggnog." His mother led the way to the family room.

Snuggled next to Sterling for the next hour or so, Ciara heard about his childhood antics.

"My son took his role as big brother seriously, even cooking them a snack if we weren't home and dinner wasn't ready," Mrs. Price spoke proudly.

"He burnt the beans." Briana scrunched her nose and shuddered as if she relived the moment. "And when Danielle and I were teenagers, Sterling would inspect our clothes to make sure they were appropriate to wear around boys, as if he was our daddy." Briana rolled her eyes.

"Sounds a lot like my dad." Ciara squinted at Sterling, recalling their earlier conversation about her father's input on the second job.

The Prices described the Sterling she had come to know. He was a protector and nourisher, and as humble as she had witnessed at Walmart in the toy section.

The night ended at her front door with the sweetest kisses and hugs that weren't on Walmart property. "You taste like apple cider." He kissed her with a passion that didn't cross the line, but she still almost collapsed in his arms.

ON MONDAY MORNING, Ciara got a dose of a reality check when she reviewed the weekend donation report for Help 100 Families.

Case number fifty-one was of great interest to her. It had received five hundred dollars combined from seven donors. Mrs. Green would stretch that amount as if it were a thousand.

Had Sterling been one of the contributors? She resisted the temptation to find out. Her interest in Sterling was no longer his donations. He was worth more to her heart than his bank account.

"Focus." With nineteen days before Christmas, more than half of Help 100 Families had been had featured. Compared to the previous year, weekly donations were down.

Where were her sympathetic donors?

Ciara might not have a lot of money, but working a second job was something she could do to contribute. The achy back, hurting feet and adjusted dinner break that was sometimes cut to forty-five minutes was worth it for thirty days. After this week, even less.

Case number forty-seven was another of the dozen cases profiled that weekend. Ciara sighed. Relationships were complicated. In her line of work, she had seen many unfavorable outcomes play out over and over. Bad marriages with abuse, children as witnesses, mothers fleeing for their lives... the final blow was losing custody of all or some children for lack of stable housing.

After five years in an abusive marriage, a young mother found the courage to leave her husband. She is living in a shelter with two of her children, ages three and seven and fear that her ex-husband will find them. She needs a permanent home and custody of her other children. A job would help her to begin her new life. Furniture, clothing, toys, and books.

Her office phone rang. "Help 100 Families. This is Ciara."

"And this is Sterling Price." He cleared his throat, and she contained her humor. "I would like to make a donation." His tone was very businesslike.

Yes! Ciara noted he hadn't made any contributions through her for a week, so this lifted her spirits. Any amount would help.

She played along on the recorded line. "Have you chosen which case or cases?"

"Three hundred dollars to case number forty-six and two hundred to case number fifty-five."

"One moment as I process your credit card information." When the transaction was complete, she thanked him on behalf of charity.

"You are most welcome, Miss Summers."

Mirth replaced his business tone as they said their goodbyes. Not a minute later, he called on her cell phone. "Hello again, beautiful."

She giggled as her heart seemed to sing. "It's good to hear your voice, even if it for business."

A call from Amber interrupted them as they discussed his company Christmas party. "Hey, my sister's calling me. Talk to you later." She ended one call and answered the other.

"Ciara, I'm nearby. Are you busy?" Amber asked.

"Never for you. Come on." She missed doing things with her sisters this time of year, but they would make it up on a ski trip next month in Colorado. It was another annual sisterhood thing they did together. They all had paid their portions, so the lodge was ready and waiting for them.

Soon, Amber waltzed into Ciara's office. The sisters hugged, then Amber removed her coat and gloves and settled in the chair. Folding her arms, she grinned and lifted a brow. "So... how was brunch? What's the latest with Sterling?"

"All good." If only Ciara could float in the air like a ballerina to describe her happiness.

"And Walmart?"

Ciara shook her head. "Girl, I'm not trying to make God mad, complaining about my feet. I'll be able to bless more families with essentials and gift cards. Plus, the signing bonus will knock off my credit card balance from my Black Friday shopping spree."

"That's doing a lot before Christmas with a new boyfriend." Amber linked her fingers together on top of Ciara's desk. "I'm glad I work in accounting from eight to four. I deal with numbers all day, not people in crisis. I don't see how you do it and not become depressed."

"Jesus. Jesus is my sanity. I'm concerned that donations are down. I'd be selfish to ignore the reason for the season—not showing compassion to those in need—and get caught up with my wants and needs. After Christmas, it will be me and Sterling all the time."

"Really?" Amber acted like she didn't believe what Ciara had said. "And he's like okay with getting your crumbs after the second job?"

Ciara grinned. "It's not that bad. He's making 'us' work. Our budding relationship stepped out of a romance novel." She waved her hands in the air and rocked in her chair as if she was at a musical concert.

"I'm happy for you. Don't want your baby sister beating you to the altar." Something outside the window seemed to grab Amber's attention.

"What? wait. You've met someone?" Ciara blinked and wiggled in her chair. "Details. Details."

"Yep. Let's just say double dating could be an option for New Year's Eve."

"Really? Wow. You did that undercover." Ciara listened as Amber described a man who sounded as wonderful as Sterling—until she mentioned he was unemployed.

"Cutbacks at Christmas." Amber shrugged as if it were no big deal. "He'll start sending out résumés in January."

Ciara didn't like the sound of the mystery man's lack of motivation. "I'll pick him up an application at Walmart."

Amber laughed as she gathered her things to leave.

"I'm serious. I never thought you would go for a man who doesn't have his own money."

"I never said he didn't have money. He was a regional sales director at a radio station. He has two cars, rental properties, and a condo. He's good." Amber winked and strutted out of Ciara's office.

"I LOVE CHRISTMASTIME," Dray said, strolling into Sterling's office wearing a red Santa hat.

Sterling looked up at him and squinted. His friend was more jolly than usual. "Me too."

"How's it going with your contributions?" Dray slipped his hands into his pants pockets.

"Made my December contributions earlier. I'll make two more and reach my goal for the year." Sterling's fingers hovered over the keyboard. He was scared to ask his business partner, who seemed to be waiting for Sterling to do just that. "What's up?"

"Glad you asked." He reached for the chair in front of Sterling's desk and made himself comfortable. "Just got off the call with Pete. He and Walt's business has climbed to second place behind Ken's, which means, we've dropped to fourth place in year-end contributions." The horror on his face was comical, but Sterling reigned in his amusement.

"It's okay—"

"We need to step up our game." Dray cut him off. "I don't like to lose, not this year when we're bringing in more revenue and can afford to give more. That being said, we're closer to the top spot than previous years."

"Bro, there are no losers in what we're doing. Look at it as a fund drive." He thought about Ciara's cases. He couldn't say the same about those families. "At the end of the day, this isn't a competition. Even with our contributions and matching our employees, we wouldn't hit number one. Our business can only do so much. We're thriving, but we're not millionaires."

"I'd say twelve thousand more dollars, and we'll beat out Kenneth's transportation empire." Dray rubbed his chin in thought.

Kenneth's transportation company had been expanding for five years straight. His small business had fifty or more employees on the payroll. Pete and Walt's engineering services were in high demand from winning minority contracts. Every Dime We Spend's services were catching on through word of mouth and targeted ad promotions. He and Dray were well on their way to the top.

"Dray, you just won us three new contracts. We're growing. I don't want our company to have to file bankruptcy because we gave too much away for the sake of a tax write-off. So please," he said, squeezing his lips in frustration, "forget about trying to outdo our frat brothers, because I'm not rescinding bonuses. Our loyal employees earned them."

"Nah." Dray rubbed his shaven head. "Listen, we're projected to have a thirty-seven percent increase in revenue next year, and we definitely will hire more staff. We got this. Let me go write another check to the Sickle Cell Association."

The partners encouraged its employees to remember their local communities when giving, if possible. "Stay within our means, bro."

"We're so close." Dray measured the distance between his thumb and finger before he stood and walked out of the office.

Sterling massaged his forehead. "Lord, please don't let this man run us out of business."

Chapter Ten

Get fired or quit. Resignation or termination. Ciara weighed her options as she rang up the next Walmart shopper at register ten.

Where was her relief?

Ciara skipped her lunch and breaks to leave an hour early to make Sterling's Christmas party. That was her only option, since none of the coworkers she knew wanted to switch shifts with her.

Spying the time, Ciara pasted on a tense smile for her customer, then paged Tanya, yet again, about her relief. With no choice, Ciara scanned the next item on the conveyor belt.

Being terminated was not an option two weeks before Christmas. She had a purpose for the extra money. Using her personal savings to buy a few more things wasn't an option. Plus, she had never gotten fired from a job, even her first job at a daycare center during her summer vacation.

Finally, with little urgency in her steps, Tanya made a pit stop at register eight to answer a question.

Lord, I'm not Lazarus that I can wait for hours for this woman to come rescue me.

"What ya need, Ciara? A void?" Tanya made her way to register ten.

Dumbfounded, Ciara kept a straight face when she wanted to cross her eyes at the woman who was slow to respond to anything—fire alarm, shoplifting threat, bathroom break. "To leave, remember? Who's my replacement?"

"I'm working on it." Tanya turned away.

"Working on it?" Ciara could feel her attitude rising. "While you do that, I'm turning off my light and closing down my lane. I hope my replacement is here before then."

Spinning around, the shift supervisor's nostrils flared as she lifted her voice. "Do that, and you're fired." Tanya didn't blink.

Oh, a standoff, huh? Ciara felt like rolling her neck but didn't. "Will that be before the next customer or when I shut it down?" Ciara's sass surprised her. This was so out of her character, especially when she believed in taking one for the team.

"After your last customer." Tanya *hmmmph*ed and shuffled away.

Ciara's heart pounded. What had she done? So many contrary thoughts ran through her mind. *You did that for a man? You did the right thing, girl, you're a professional, You don't have to take that,* and... *Don't do it. Those families will benefit from what you're doing for them to survive.*

She had checked out a shopper for the last time. Ciara turned off her light and said to her customer, "Sorry, someone else will check you out."

No turning back now. With forty minutes to get home, shower, and get dressed, Ciara didn't waste any time clocking out for the last time at Walmart.

"You'll receive your last check next Thursday, but you just blew your two hundred bucks signing bonus." Tanya escorted her out to the entrance to make sure she didn't go ballistic like the employee who was fired the week before, or to make sure

Ciara didn't shoplift any merchandise like another guy Tanya fired two days ago.

During the drive home, Ciara felt numb, questioning her actions. It sunk in that she'd lost wages. *I hope you're worth it, Mr. Price.*

Ciara pulled into her driveway. Jessica was sitting in her car. She jumped out and marched to Ciara's car.

"A woman should never rush for a party. You're not leaving much time for hair and makeup…" Jessica fussed.

"Sorry." She turned the lock in the door and walked inside. Jessica trailed her. "I'm going to shower. Let Amber in when she arrives, then I'll tell both of you that I quit."

"Huh?" Jessica's eyes popped, and her jaw dropped. "You never quit something you start."

"Who quit?" Amber asked as she pushed the door open.

"Details after my shower." Ciara disappeared upstairs to her bedroom. She grabbed her things and hurried into the bathroom.

Fifteen minutes later, she stepped into her room and glanced at the long cream dress with gold embellishments on the bed, borrowed from Jessica. Her sisters sat on the other side of it, swinging their legs.

"Talk," Amber said. "Something must have happened for you to quit, even if it was Walmart."

Ciara shrugged and fingered the evening dress. "Sterling's company Christmas party started a half hour ago. I asked to get off early. It wasn't going to happen. I had to make a choice. I chose Sterling."

"Yes! She chose Sterling," Amber said, and high-fived Jessica.

"Wow. You quit." Jessica stared in awe, then grinned.

"I did." Ciara chuckled, then took her seat in front of the vanity. "Now, ladies, make me beautiful."

"SO WHERE IS THIS PRINCESS Ciara you've been boasting about? Got you wearing suits to work." Dray raised his brows, then craned his neck, looking around the hotel ballroom. "I thought she would be on your arm."

He shoved Sterling, then gulped down whatever alcohol was in his glass.

Boasting was never good. If he was *stupid*-stitious, doing so would be a sure to jinx anything. Sterling wasn't.

Still, he avoided boasting at all costs because of another life lesson he learned in Tempe, Arizona. On the football field, Sterling was fearless as a linebacker and boasted nonstop about his skills. The devil incited Sterling's opponents to challenge him. Sterling hadn't seen the hit coming that cost him to miss two games and shut up.

God had reminded him of First Corinthians 1:31: *if anyone boasts, let him boast of the Lord*, and Scripture after Scripture about humility. Sterling never forgot—neither did his shoulder. Yes, he was excited about Ciara and singing her praises. Not boasting. There was a difference.

"She'll be here. Ciara had to work." Sterling smiled and nodded at passing employees. "You know how women are, probably running late."

Dray rocked on his heels. "You told me she's a social worker. They work on Saturday evenings? I guess they're on the clock twenty-four seven."

"Actually, Ciara's hours are set. She's working a second job at Walmart." Sterling hadn't meant to tell his friend that.

Oh, well. It was frustration talking. What mattered to Sterling was Ciara wasn't with him, holding his hand and snuggling close to him with her enchanting smile.

Dray didn't mask his pity. "A second job. Wow, I don't know if I'm impressed for her to take responsibility for her cash fund or sorry for you that you might be stood up and—"

Angela Forman, the company's talented graphic designer, strolled up to the men wearing a shimmering red dress. Dray gawked and forgot what he was about to say. It was probably something that Sterling didn't want to hear.

It was no secret Angela had a crush on Dray. Although his friend didn't encourage the attraction, tonight might change that.

Sterling was amused. He understood allure. He felt it instantly when he met Ciara in person. She had resuscitated his heart, which had momentarily stopped pumping.

Where was she? The party had been underway for about forty minutes. Sterling was about to call her when an employee approached him.

He groaned. Not Stephanie.

Stephanie possessed a wealth of knowledge about diverse subjects, but she was long-winded. Sterling had no choice but to entertain her for a few minutes.

"Do you remember my husband, Jake, who happens to work for State Farm as an agent?" She giggled.

Only Stephanie thought that fact was hilarious.

Sterling half listened as he wondered why Ciara had to work when she told him that she could switch her shift. Last night, she broke the news that she couldn't and apologized, but insisted she would get off in time to come. Now what?

Lord, don't let me have to go down to Walmart and get my woman.

Chapter Eleven

If her sisters didn't stop their primping, Ciara wasn't going to make the Christmas party. She seldom bothered with fancy hairstyles because it took too much effort. Like now.

Strand by strand, Jessica framed spiral curls around Ciara's face. "Now that's sophistication. You look like a princess."

Both sisters eyed Ciara's reflection in the bathroom mirror.

In awe, Ciara stared at her transformation. Amber had somehow concealed the tiredness around Ciara's eyes with makeup. "I do look different."

"My dress was made for your curves." Jessica patted Ciara's shoulder.

"And your gold slippers." Amber placed her four- or five-inch heels before Ciara.

She slipped her feet into the stilettos, wiggled her toes, and stood.

They were gorgeous, but her feet protested for something more comfortable. She would have to suffer the punishment, so not to hurt her sister's feeling. Amber and Jessica were having fun dressing her up.

Amber fastened a hand on her hip and *tsk*ed. "Remember, they're designer shoes."

"I won't." Ciara stole another glimpse at her reflection. "I feel like royalty. Cinderella—the Black one, of course."

When they FaceTimed their mother, she suggested Ciara wear one of her tiaras she had won as volunteer of the year at some function.

"That would be overkill, Mama. It's a Christmas party, not a gala," Ciara had told them.

Jessica tapped her chin in thought. "All you need is a chariot, a Clydesdale or limo...."

Amber high-fived their oldest sister and bobbed her head. "You definitely need to ride, not drive to this shindig, and I don't mean Uber. What princess drives herself to an affair?"

"Me." Ciara waved her sister off. "It's not a big production, but a small company party."

"You can't. You'll ruin my reputation." Amber feigned horror. "You're representing the Summers girls." She wiggled a brow. Some mischievous plot was stirring in her head. "I bet if you called Sterling right now, he would stop what he's doing and come running for his queen."

"I'm a princess, remember? But he's the host. What host leaves their own party?" Ciara joked.

"Jesus left his ninety-nine sheep to go after the one," Amber said out of the blue.

"Not the same. That was about salvation," Ciara reminded her.

"Sis, any man who brings his woman dinner to Walmart will leave his own party to get you. Call Sterling. Tonight is your Night of Miracles, Cinderella ball, and everything Christmas."

"You've got a point." Their excitement was convincing. She tapped Sterling's name on her phone.

"Ciara? Are you here or on your way? Where are you?" He skipped hello and asked off one question after another. "Please tell me you're not still at work." He didn't hide the panic in his voice—or maybe it was irritation.

"I'm not." Was she the cause of his anxiety? Feeling horrible, Ciara gnawed on her lip, and Jessica slapped Ciara's finger away from her mouth.

"Do you want lipstick on her your teeth?" her sister fussed in a low voice.

"I'm dressed and ready to go..." She thought again about adding more stress on the host leaving his own function. He had gone out of his way for her more than once. She couldn't bring herself to demand one more thing.

"Chicken." Jessica rolled her eyes.

"Really, just ask the man." Amber gritted her teeth and reached for Ciara's phone.

Ciara blocked her attempt. "If one of my sisters drops me off, will you bring me home? I mean, it's hard to drive in these heels." She planned to take the heels off when she was out of their eyesight and go barefooted the rest of the night if she had to.

"You don't have to ask, baby. You're my date, and I never wanted you to drive anyway. I'm on my way."

Jessica and Amber's sighs were in sync as they did happy dances to celebrate a win in Ciara's favor. "He's coming for his woman." Jessica started the chant and Amber joined in.

Ciara laughed at them, happy that Sterling didn't mind coming for her. She grabbed her purse and held on to the banister, taking each step down with caution to keep from injuring herself in those shoes. Both sisters trailed her, lifting the hem of her dress as if it were the train of a wedding dress.

Sterling arrived sooner than expected, wearing a red fedora and a long black coat. His precise stride against the backdrop of the snow shower made Ciara wish she could capture the image and download it as a screensaver on all her devices.

"Wow." Jessica blinked.

"Don't let Justin hear you say that." Amber elbowed her sister.

"I think you two can leave now." Ciara opened her door as Sterling was about to ring her doorbell.

Sterling patted his chest. "You look more beautiful each time I see you."

Jessica snickered. "Come on, Amber. Our job here is done."

Sterling kept his eyes on Ciara as the two said their goodbyes.

Ciara swallowed, then bit her bottom lip. Lipstick beware. "I hope I'm not overdressed."

"Wow. I'm the one underdressed," he said of his black tux, then grunted. "You can dress up for me anytime."

She didn't fight her blush and was about to close the door when he suggested she might need her coat. "Oh, yeah." Ciara did so without inviting him in and grabbed her sneakers by the door and stuffed them in her bag since her sisters had left. With her wrap over her shoulders, she locked the door.

Accepting his hand, Ciara steadied herself in the heels, then she noticed her sisters were in their cars, watching her night unfold.

"Thank you." His voice was like a warm whisper as he patiently waited as she maneuvered the steps to the walkway. His grip was strong. She wouldn't fall.

When he opened his passenger door, headlights flashed on behind them. Jessica honked and pulled off first, followed by Amber.

"Sorry." She apologized for her sisters' antics.

"I have two sisters, too, remember, but only one is here to get in my business." He waited for her to click the seatbelt over her chest.

Once he was behind the wheel, the atmosphere shifted between them. Although she and Sterling had done things together before tonight, it felt like a first date. "Can I tell you something?"

"Of course." He bobbed his head, checked his rearview mirror, and drove away from the curb. "Anything."

"I quit my second job this evening. My boss may have had another take on us parting ways. It depends on whose version you want to believe."

"Yours." He faced her in slow motion. She could see a hint of a grin despite his concerned expression. "Why?"

"It's okay to laugh." Ciara chuckled.

And he did. Uncontrollably until he snickered, then he sobered. "Okay," he said, taking a deep breath, "now that that's out of the way, what happened?"

"I didn't want to miss your Christmas party. I made an executive decision. If I hadn't, I'd probably still be at work waiting on my relief. It was non-stop shoppers all day."

"Woman, you just made my day. Remind me to kiss you at the next stoplight. Nah." He wrinkled his nose. "I won't forget."

Sterling didn't let go of her hand as he carefully maneuvered the wet road until they arrived a half hour later to the Moonrise Hotel. "I can't wait to show off my princess."

"Thank you for making me feel so special." She would have to think of something sweet to do for him. Oh, this was so worth quitting her job. A party. Food. And a prince.

LINKING HIS FINGERS through Ciara's, Sterling entered the hotel lobby with a little swag in his step. With Ciara on his arm, he felt complete.

He didn't need a red carpet to show off his regal date. *Thank You, Jesus, I didn't have to wait until Christmas to receive my blessing.*

As they cleared the entrance to the banquet room, Sterling spotted Dray speaking with one of their employees.

One glance at Sterling, Dray stopped holding court with their guests and made quick steps to Sterling and Ciara, where they waited, as if they were about to be announced for a coronation.

"Where'd you go, man?" Dray grinned, admiring Ciara.

"To pick up my lady. Ciara Summers, meet my business partner, Dray Blakely. We're like brothers."

"It's nice to meet you, Dray," she said as Sterling removed her wrap to reveal a dress that sculpted her figure.

This would certainly be the best Christmas ever. Sterling patted his chest to comfort his heart rate.

"I'm glad you could make it, working two jobs—"

"Bye, Dray." Sterling frowned, then steered Ciara away from his friend to their table.

Ciara's financial distress wasn't Dray's business, and Sterling should have never mentioned it to him.

His date didn't seem to hear as she glanced around the room in awe. "Wow. You go all out. Whoever did your decorations should be commended."

Ciara pointed to the red, green, and gold metallic balloons that were manipulated into arches positioned in two corners of the room. A tower of gift boxes was centered inside both.

Wrapping his arm around her waist, she leaned into him as he steered her toward one of the displays. "Party Decor is one of our clients, and they do an outstanding job."

"Are all those gifts for your employees?" She looked up into his eyes, and all he could think about was kissing her lips.

When Ciara blinked, Sterling kissed the tip of her nose instead. This wasn't the setting for anything more, but she would tempt him all night. That he was sure of. "Ah, yes—and charity. Our company is small—thirteen employees but growing. We started with Dray, me and my parents as unpaid employees. We hope to add three positions next month. Two might be remote."

If the Lord's wills it, his company might even double the number of employees before the end of next year. Although, they planned to bring on a couple in January.

Sterling nodded and waved to his employees, who seemed enthralled with his date, as he made the rounds of introductions, then guided Ciara toward the buffet. They helped themselves to a selection of meats, sides, and bread.

Until Ciara arrived, Sterling didn't have much of an appetite. Now, he was famished.

"I hope I don't stretch my sister's dress overindulging." Ciara chuckled as she stacked an assortment of sweets on her dessert plate.

Sterling scanned her figure. "Never. If there's a thread out of place, I'll personally take you shopping to replace the dress."

So, she borrowed the clothes instead of buying an ensemble on a credit card. That made Sterling smile.

"What? Sterling Price wants to go shopping—with me?" Her eyes sparkled with a tease. Her lips curled into a smile.

This woman tested his resolve to be respectable when he wanted to scoop her up in his arms, find a hiding place, and smother her with kisses. *Tame your emotions and hormones, Price.*

After an imaginary salute, he cleared his throat. "As long as it's not outside in a tent." He escorted her to their table, where meticulous Christmas centerpieces were on display.

He took their plates and laid them on the table, then pulled out her chair.

Sterling scooted his seat closer, took Ciara's hand, then gave thanks. Moments after, employee Nita and her husband, Warren, appeared. She wore a long blue dress, and Warren sported a blue bowtie.

She introduced herself and her husband to Ciara, then complimented the party. "Ciara, I've never seen my boss so happy." She giggled. "Oh, by the way, Sterling, you and Dray outdid yourselves tonight."

"Thanks for both compliments."

When the couple left, Ciara touched his hand. "I'm happy too. I've never felt so cherished and special. I don't believe in the magic of Christmas, so I'll say being with you has been incredible."

"I agree." Sterling puffed out his chest. "Is the food good?"

She nodded, covering her mouth as she chewed. Next, Ciara dabbed her lips. "Scrumptious."

"Ciara, I know how important that second job was to you, and I don't take it lightly for choosing me over the loss of wages." That made him emotional.

"You're important to me too." She leaned closer, and he met her. They kissed, brief but the spark seemed to burn his lips.

When her lashes fluttered open, Ciara gave him a smile that melted his heart like chocolate at a fondue bar. "Are you enjoying yourself?"

"Yes. I'm glad I'm not overdressed."

"Your beauty has never disappointed me from the first moment I saw you." He made her blush, and he liked having the power to do that. "Since you're seemingly available now, and it's fifteen days before Christmas, how about filling up our calendar with holiday dates?"

She tilted her head, eyes sparkling, and studied him. "Please tell me it's not going to be like the twelve days of Christmas. I don't need a partridge in a pear tree, turtle doves or gold rings."

Rings? Getting to know Ciara had him thinking long term. Who knew? This time next year, she might get a ring.

"What else do you have planned?"

Dray popped up from nowhere. He leaned over Sterling's shoulder. "Ready to do this, man?"

Oh, yeah. Although handing out the bonuses was the favorite part of the program, Sterling couldn't wait to get it over with and get back to Ciara.

He stood, never taking his eyes off her. He hoped she would miss his presence as he would hers for the brief minutes apart. "Excuse us, babe. We need to hand out the Christmas bonuses."

"Incredible." Ciara's mouth formed an "o," and her eyes watered. "Gifts and bonuses, Sterling? Our charity was fortunate to be on your radar this year."

"I think you and I were on God's radar to find each other." Sterling thought about the challenge he and other Black entrepreneurs faced to give back to their local communities. A commitment that Dray had wanted to take to the extreme, but at the end of the day, the success of their business meant everything to Dray and Sterling. "Jesus is the reason for this season."

Ciara applauded his employees as if she knew them personally when their names were called to receive their bonus.

A cheerleader? Sterling smiled as Dray took the microphone and called the last of the employees.

"Merry Christmas, team. Sterling and I appreciate everything you do for the business. Make sure you grab an extra gift under the arches for someone else."

Sterling nodded to the disc jockey to turn up the Christmas music, and he rejoined Ciara, who was yawning, but her face glowed when their eyes met.

For the rest of the night, Sterling was content to have Ciara in his arms, resting against his chest. He spied sneakers on her feet and chuckled. Where did she get those? So that's what she had in the decorative bag she carried.

He studied her lashes as her chest rose with a faint snore. Beautiful. He kissed her curls and glanced around, a content man, while Dray danced with the single ladies in a circle.

When the music stopped, Ciara stretched. "Sorry. I closed my eyes. I kept you from enjoying your own party." She pouted.

He placed a finger on her lips. "I have no complaints. I think Dray danced enough for both of us. Although I'd like to kidnap you for the night, I'd better get you home." Sterling linked her fingers through his as he helped her stand and get her things, then they said their good nights to others.

Outside, an inch of snow greeted them.

"Careful," he said as he helped her into his vehicle. Too soon, they arrived at her house. She turned to him, smiled, and pressed a kiss on his cheek, then seemed to admire her handiwork.

"I like the color red on you." Ciara giggled as she rubbed off her lipstick.

"I happen to like it better on your lips." He cupped her chin and brought her lips to his, and they shared a sweet goodnight kiss.

At her door, he pulled her closer. "By the way, nice sneakers. Thank you for coming into my life. You've got me thinking about settling down with a beautiful wife and children..." He didn't say more as he watched her reaction.

Lost for words, Ciara closed her eyes and waited for his kiss, which he delivered with a passion he never felt before. Before he lost control, it was as if a hand on his shoulder pulled him back.

Sterling opened his eyes, panted, and looked around, expecting to see someone like her father. There was no one there, but Sterling knew for a fact, there was a hand on his shoulder, pulling him away from going too far with passion that could turn into lust without him realizing it.

After more pecks on her soft lips, Sterling said good night. With each step, he walked away, wondering if he had said too much.

Chapter Twelve

"Jessica, is it possible to be in love after one kiss? I mean, it wasn't our first, but it felt different—kind of." Ciara rambled over the speakerphone, giddy as she dressed to attend Sterling's church. So far, they were alternating visits to each other's churches.

A good night's rest made her dream about a forever with Sterling.

Ciara's imagination was in full force. That's why she hadn't mentioned what Sterling said about settling down to her sister.

Because he was speaking in general, she reasoned. Not this soon.

"Hmmm." Her sister giggled. "I fell for Justin early. Our first kiss sealed the deal, and our feelings grew from there. Your feelings are strong for Sterling. You quit your job for him."

"Not quite. It was a part-time seasonal job. There's a difference," Ciara clarified with a jut of her chin. "Plus, he invited me before I got hired, and I forgot to request the time off. When Tanya wouldn't let me off early after she had signed off on it, I walked."

"Girl, stop fighting it. You and Sterling are perfect for each other."

Ciara blushed, then released the grin. "I think so too." They spoke a few more minutes before ending the call. There was no need to call Amber because her sisters tag-teamed each other with updates about the "Sterling affair."

She didn't care what they labeled her relationship. Ciara was happy about her decision to quit, but she debated whether she wanted to find another temporary position two weeks before Christmas or make holiday memories with Sterling. Hands down, Mr. Price won her affections. He even uttered the taboo words a man said to a woman: *Thinking about settling down.*

That wasn't a marriage proposal, and who did that anyway in less than a month of dating?

Half an hour later, Ciara opened her front door to Sterling. His eyes flashed a happiness that filled her heart.

He leaned over and brushed his lips against hers. "Good morning."

After she locked the door, Ciara slipped her hand in his, and they walked to his vehicle. They stayed connected throughout the ride up to when they arrived at House of Blessings. Once they knelt to pray inside the sanctuary to give thanks for another day and took their seats, their hands found each other again.

When Pastor Franklin stood at the podium, he smiled. "We're in the season of giving, saints of God."

Ciara exchanged glances with Sterling. "That's how we met." She squeezed his hand.

Sterling winked. Before she could flirt back, his pastor pulled them in with the Scripture.

"In Second Corinthians 9: 6-7, the Bible says, '*But this I say, He which sows sparingly shall reap also sparingly; and he which sows bountifully shall reap also bountifully.*'"

The pastor nodded. "*Every man according as he purposes in his heart, so let him give; not grudgingly, or of necessity: for God loves a cheerful giver.*' My sermon today is 'What's Your Purpose in Giving? And why does there need to be a season to give?' According to nonprofits, thirty percent of donations occur between Thanksgiving and the end of the year."

Ciara and Sterling both nodded, and she said, "True."

"I challenge everyone here to be a cheerful giver after December thirty-first. Give to others less fortunate like every day is Christmas..."

Ciara couldn't preach the message any better. The sermon was a campaign poster for her charity and all agencies that serviced the poor. She talked back to the pastor with several "Amens" along with others until he concluded his sermon.

"I did kinda go overboard buying for those in need this year. I don't need any of that stuff."

Sterling stared at her with a slacked jaw. Whatever he was about to say was thwarted when all the attention was on three teenagers walking down the aisle from somewhere in the back, responding to accept the call for salvation. Ciara's heart lifted. They weren't dressed for church. Any other place, they would be out of their element, but in God's house, there was room for sinners and saints.

One by one, the three received prayer. Two returned to their seats, but one repented with so much emotion that he slid to his knees, crying out for Jesus to forgive and save him.

Ciara stood in her pew to support him from afar. She connected with the young man's emotional release, which she experienced when she surrendered her life to Christ. The scene triggered an avalanche around the sanctuary of people wanting to seek God.

There was nonstop traffic to the altar, and Ciara realized there were five baptismal candidates who had entered the pool behind the choir stand.

A hush swept over the auditorium as the teenager descended into the water dressed in a clean white T-shirt, pants, and socks. He had started the procession to the altar, so it wasn't surprising he was the first to be baptized.

"My dear brother, upon your repentance and the confession of your faith and the confidence that we have in the blessed Word of God, concerning His death, burial and grand resurrection, I now indeed baptize you in the name of Jesus Christ for the remission of your sins because there is no name under heaven by which man can be saved. And He promises to give you His spirit with the evidence of speaking in other tongues."

The young man was submerged and reappeared, rejoicing as praises filled the sanctuary. The Spirit was high, and folks shouted praises to the Lord; others dance while many prayed.

Ciara noticed the other two teenagers had returned to the altar, wanting what their friend had received—forgiveness and the Holy Ghost. No one in the audience left as the power of God stirred the atmosphere.

"*Whew.* I don't know about you, but I'm glad I witnessed God move mightily in this place. I worked up an appetite." Sterling patted his stomach after the pastor announced the benediction.

It had been a perfect weekend—the Christmas party and Sunday worship.

Ciara was content.

Happy.

Sterling chose Juniper in the Central West End to eat, and the place was packed when they arrived. They didn't care about a thirty-minute wait. They were in their own world.

When their table was ready, Ciara glanced out the window at the falling snow. "It snows a lot when we're together." She blushed. "I think it's romantic."

He stared into her eyes. "I'm waiting to win the snowball fight."

"*Humph.* Says the man who can't stay all night in a tent." Ciara paused. "Last night, you mentioned wanting a family. You were brave to say that to a single woman. You know those are 'let's pick out the ring, wedding dress and a date' kind of words."

"I ain't scared." He toyed with his mustache. "I blame you for putting those ideas in my head. I care about you, and I don't see that changing."

"I care about you too." Nodding, Ciara fingered the remnants of curls from her updo the night before. Bliss.

Ciara looked into his eyes until the server approached for their order. Afterward, Sterling's stare was intense, as if he was debating whether to say more or wait for her to speak. She was content to play with intertwined fingers.

The server returned in no time with Sterling's shrimp and grits and a fried chicken biscuit. Ciara played it safe with two blueberry hoe cakes with blackberry-mint syrup.

Sterling reached for her hands again and squeezed. "Lord, thank You for this incredible meal and this special woman You placed in my life. Please bless and sanctify it to Your glory and help us to bless those who are hungry. In Jesus' name. Amen."

"Amen."

Sampling each other's food had become the norm, so they took no prisoners as they dived in.

"You know, the message and the service today were amazing. I'm so glad we were together to witness the movement of God." Sterling smiled.

"Yes, me too." Ciara slipped another morsel of her cake in her mouth.

"But you dropped a bombshell on me after the pastor's sermon. Those gifts are for families in need? Wow. I had no idea." He shook his head and chuckled. "I admire you for sowing abundantly because that's in your heart." He paused and stroked his beard. "At first, I thought you needed some serious intervention. I've never seen a woman shop so much. I'm glad you quit that job, although you had a spending addiction for a worthy cause."

His chuckle turned into a hearty laugh before he reached for another shrimp and slid it into his mouth.

Hmmm. An addict? That hurt. Her good mood fled the premises. Ciara rested her fork and twisted her lips. "Did you just insult me? Are you my intervention officer?" She shot daggers from her eyes, hoping they would turn into fireballs. But tears threatened to extinguish them.

Sterling frowned. "No, baby. Wait, I didn't mean it like that..." he stuttered. "I can show you how to budget, so you won't need to work second jobs, especially around Christmas. I'd much rather you spend time with me."

Ciara lifted a brow. "For your information, I don't need to work an extra job every year. I don't look at my giving as an addiction, but a sacrifice. It's not about money, but families. I thought you understood my passion." Ciara took a deep breath and exhaled. Her feelings were hurt that he'd attacked her character.

She huffed and folded her arms. "And for your information, I have two savings accounts, a high-interest earning checking account, and a couple of CDs. I have a Christmas bank account set aside for such a time as this."

Ciara was hot. She had a good first impression of him. Why did his have to be bad of her? "I'm thirty-three years old. My father made sure all his daughters were capable of money management. I don't need your budget advice." Shaking her head, Ciara scooted back from the table.

At the moment, Sterling couldn't fix this. Ciara stood, and on shaky legs walked out to the lobby to cool off. It didn't help. She became more annoyed.

She wasn't going back there, knowing he thought so little of her. *I can't believe I quit my job—albeit Walmart—for this man.* She swallowed as she texted Amber.

Hey, I'm at Juniper's in the U-City Loop. Can you come and get me as soon as possible? I'll explain when you get here.

It took a minute for Amber to text back, but it seemed like forever. **What? Bad timing. I just popped some popcorn for me and Tristan, but we're on our way. You owe me!**

Who's Tristan? **Thanks, but don't bring him. I'm about to cry, and it won't be pretty.**

Her heart was aching because against her better judgment, she was attracted to a man who felt she needed saving. That was the risk she took going out with him, thanks to Amber and Jessica.

She spied Sterling paying the server. Ciara slipped into the ladies' restroom to wait until Amber arrived—twenty minutes, at least. Hopefully, other patrons would have a short visit. Sterling called. She sent him to voicemail and turned down the volume. Next, came his texts of apology. Ciara ignored them. She had to get over her hurt.

Then she heard his voice outside the door. "Excuse me, miss. I'm looking for my girlfriend. Can you see if there is a Ciara Summers inside?"

"O-okay," a squeaky voice of a young woman said.

Ciara scrambled inside a stall and closed the door as the woman called out her name a couple of times.

The woman said, "Sorry, sir. No one answered."

Sterling texted again. **Where are you? Are you okay?**

Ciara twisted her lips. **I'm okay, Sterling. Go home. I can't talk to you right now.** *Come on, Amber.*

Twenty-eight minutes later, Amber texted her to come out. Ciara opened the door, and a woman bounced back.

They exchanged apologies as Ciara made a beeline for the exit without looking over her shoulder for Sterling. In addition to Amber, Jessica was in the front seat. Ciara slid in the back. "Home, please. Hurry. Now."

"Girl, I hope you don't have to use the bathroom the way you're rushing Amber." Jessica glanced over her shoulder. "What happened?"

"I should have never let my guard down and gone out with Sterling." She sniffed before the dam broke. "I thought he understood my passion for the families I serve, but no, he said I had an addiction when it came to shopping."

"Addiction?" Amber rolled her neck. "That's not nice. Do we need to do a drive-by at his house? I already have an attitude about Tristan and my movie marathon. We were about to play movie trivia." Amber gritted her teeth and gripped the steering wheel as if she was taking a driver's test instead of her usual relaxed one-hand steering.

"Who's Tristan?" Ciara and Jessica said in unison.

Amber waved them off. "Next time. This is Ciara's drama now."

"Why did I have to really like him?" Ciara bawled, mad at herself for falling for him.

"Because he was a perfect match for you, sis," Jessica said softly.

"Who breaks up with a new girlfriend before Christmas?" Amber asked.

When Jessica cut her eyes at Amber, Ciara squared her shoulders and leaned forward. "Ah, technically, I broke up with him. I walked away." She'd done a lot of breaking up this weekend. First the job and now the man.

"Clearly, the discussion isn't over. I think that's his car sitting in your driveway." Jessica pointed when they pulled up to her house.

"I told him to go home. Keep going," Ciara ordered.

"If I keep going, you're going back to my house where Tristan is waiting for me." Amber lifted her brow. "Your choice. Choose your house."

"Sis, you might as well hear him out, as he digs himself out of a hole, then you can put him out." Jessica winked.

Reluctantly, Ciara stepped out and watched her sisters drive away. Really? They stayed to see them off to the party and now, they were leaving her to fend for herself?

Ciara spun around and headed for her front door. She didn't stop as he got out of his car and trailed her. "Merry Christmas, Sterling, and have a Happy New Year."

"Not without you." His voice was low, which made her glance over her shoulder.

"Sterling, we've been seeing each other for three weeks. If I had known that you thought I was an addict, we wouldn't have made it past three days. I work with cases of recovering addicts. They are struggling to overcome. That's not me. Can't believe you thought that or said it."

She entered her house and waited for Sterling to knock on her door or ring the bell. He did neither. After a few minutes, Ciara heard his engine start, then him driving away.

A tear fell, then another. She wasn't the one he was dreaming of settling down with. Who could she blame for this disaster?

Satan, God whispered.

Now, Ciara was really mad. She had allowed the devil to steal her joy.

Chapter Thirteen

After a fitful night, Sterling woke the next morning ticked, clueless, and hurt about Ciara's behavior. What was she angry about?

He needed a sounding board. Thomas Price was not only Sterling's father, but a confidant. He called his dad on his drive to the office for insight.

"Son, if Ciara has you this flustered after a disagreement, then she means something to you. You might even love her. The best thing to do is apologize."

Sterling shook his head as if his father could see him. "Ciara should have returned to the table, so we could clear the misunderstanding. She blew what I said out of proportion, then she called her sisters for a pickup as if I had left her stranded. That hurt." Then she slammed her front door. That crushed him. The more he thought about it, she owed him an apology. He grunted. "I'm not feeling that."

"Son, what does the Bible say about our mouths? James 3:7–8 says, '*Man can tame all kinds of animals, birds, reptiles, and creatures of the sea, but no man can tame the tongue. It is a restless evil, full of deadly poison.*'"

That gave Sterling pause. Yes, he knew that Scripture, which was why he ended his morning prayers with, *"Let the words of my mouth and meditation of my heart be acceptable to You, Oh Lord, my Strength and Redeemer,"* paraphrasing Psalm 19:14.

He tried to be careful in his words, but failed this time with the woman he loved. Sterling sighed heavily, not liking how the conversation was going. It was making him look bad.

"You and Ciara are blowing this out of portion," his mother said, listening on speaker.

"I thought we were at the point we could share our thoughts and laugh about things. There was no malice behind my words."

The more Sterling's parents tried to reason with him but seemed to take Ciara's side, the more tension increased in his head. When was the last time he had a headache?

"Well, I made it to work, so I'll talk to you and Mom later." He ended the call and took a deep breath as he climbed out of his Jeep. With each step toward the building, Sterling attempted to clear his head.

"Hey, Sterling! Great party, Boss." An employee called out as she danced to her desk to the beat of the Hallelujah chorus with a mug full of java.

"Wow, boss. I didn't know you had it in you. Your girlfriend is fine." Jeff, his research guru, held the last note as if he was in the choir. He offered a fist bump. Sterling barely touched it.

He hurried past Dray's office but backtracked when his friend called out to him.

"Whoa. What happened to you, bro?"

Sterling huffed and leaned against the doorframe. "I think Ciara and I had our first fight—that is one stubborn woman. I can't believe she was working a second job to help families in Help 100 Families," he said more to himself than his friend as he threw his arms in the air. "I don't have enough space in my head right now to figure her out."

"You'd better recharge your batteries because you two looked cozy at the party. Fix it. Give the woman what she wants, and you'll both be happy."

"Right."

Sterling continued to his office. He was reviewing the new contracts when his sister's ringtone interrupted him. He needed a break even before he got started on his work.

"Hi, Danielle." He smiled for the first time that morning. "Can't wait to see you for the holidays."

"Yeah, me too, but I was looking forward to meeting Ciara. According to Mom, Ciara has turned you into a love-struck teenager, but you messed that up."

Me? They both huffed in sync. Danielle in frustration. Him in irritation as he twisted his lips. "Sorry to disappoint ya, little sis."

"If you like her, don't be so stubborn. Talk to her."

Why did everyone think it was his fault? "Don't know if I can."

"You can, big brother, and you will. Pick your poison, or me, Mama, and Briana are going to have women at your doorstep within twenty-four hours, then the blind dates will begin. Dad and Mama say Ciara is the one...."

Sterling groaned. He wasn't in the mood for this nonsense. "If you called to beat up on your brother, then I'll talk to you later."

"Okay, okay. Sorry." Danielle sounded repentant, so he relaxed.

Within minutes, every subject Danielle approached reminded him of Ciara—from her need to finish shopping to planning fun family activities when she was in town until they ended the call.

Sterling checked the time. Without a second job, unless Ciara accepted one in the middle of the night, which wouldn't surprise him, she should be home this evening. Nothing was certain, so Sterling texted her.

Blessed are the peacemakers. I'm trying to make peace and apologize. My peace offering is dinner. See you about six?

Okay.

He stopped by his home to freshen up before getting carryout. Sterling rang Ciara's doorbell twenty minutes later and waited. He exhaled the frigid air from his nostrils and kicked the layer of snow from the heel of his shoes.

Ciara opened the door and stepped aside for him to enter. He didn't know if he could collect a kiss or not, so he grinned and held up the sack. "Culver's."

"Thank you." She acted shy.

Was she as miserable too? She gave nothing away as she led him back into her kitchen.

Sterling took a seat and watched her body language. Her shoulders slumped as if she carried a heavy weight. On her toes, Ciara reached into the cabinet for plates. If she wasn't mad at him, he would have assisted and been rewarded with hugs and kisses. When she returned to the table, he couldn't dismiss her wounded expression.

Sterling stilled her hand. "I'm sorry you feel I insulted you. That wasn't my intention. I let past experiences with women and money cloud my judgment and rule my tongue without think-ing."

She nodded and gave him a smile. "Accepted. I'm sorry too."

Relief lifted his heart, so he stood and lifted her in his arms. When they sealed the apology with a kiss, he placed her feet back on the floor. "I feel better now. You changed my life, lady. My appetite has returned."

He grinned as he pulled out her chair, then retook his. "Let's eat." He cupped her hands in his and swallowed the emotion that had lodged there all day. "Lord, thank You for mending us and blessing our food. Please remove the impurities and help us to remember to feed those who are hungry. In Jesus' name. Amen."

"Sterling?" Ciara wouldn't look at him as she drew circles in her ketchup with a fry.

"Yeah, baby?"

She glanced up, and her eyes were bright. "I know I may seem like I go above and beyond, but I want to do my part, and not expect others to do all the giving. There are more families who need help besides those profiled in the paper and online."

He rested his hand on hers. "Let me contact my vendors to fill in the gaps. We are a village."

"That would be wonderful." She squeezed his hand and looked away. Suddenly, shyness draped Ciara. "I was online to-day looking for another job."

Shaking his head, Sterling said, "Why doesn't that surprise me? Just kidding. No, I'm not." He leaned forward and made up for the kisses they had missed.

"I know we've talked about a lot of things, except my past relationships. I think I'm a generous man."

"And you are." The sincerity was in her eyes.

"Thank you, but my previous girlfriends saw me as a bank, bleeding money for their heart's desires. All they saw was dollar signs, not my heart."

"In full disclosure, that's what got my attention. Don't take this the wrong way. I thought the same thing myself: Here's a man with money. A generous donor who I hoped would empty your pockets—for a cause."

Sterling felt his irritation rising. Either he didn't like the way Ciara said it or the way it sounded to his ears. "So, you were after my money too."

What was wrong with people? First, Dray was willing to go for broke. Now, the woman he cared about admitted she was using him? He had to tame his emotion.

"Yes—I mean no."

Ciara's answer didn't appease him. "What do you mean?" He frowned.

"I'm a social worker and on the board for Help 100 Families. Of course, I'm seeking donations. That's my purpose."

Humph. Her purpose, huh? "So going out with me was a way to milk me out of every dime and dollar for a cause?"

Folding her arms, Ciara lifted a brow. "Not once did I ask you to donate to a particular case or say how much to give. Of course, I was hoping and praying that you would be generous, but it's against company policy to influence a donor. I held to that when I agreed to go out with you."

Sterling rubbed his head in frustration. "You may not have verbally broken the rules, but like a sucker, you charmed me and at first, I did give more to impress you. I can't believe I admitted to that. But my intentions with you were always honest." He bit his lip for saying more than he planned.

Suddenly, Ciara had nothing more to say as her eyes watered.

Oh no. He wasn't going to fall for the tears act.

No longer hungry, Sterling stood, snatched his coat off the wall hook, and stormed out of her house. To say more would only cause him regret and repentance because he really wanted Ciara to be the one.

He was near his car when a snowball hit his back. He spun around.

"You like snowball fights, take that." Ciara went back inside and slammed her door.

Women.

Chapter Fourteen

It had been two days since Ciara threw a snowball at Sterling—petty, but she didn't miss. But she hadn't spoken to him either. Maybe he was injured.

"I forgave you. You can't forgive me?" She *tsk*ed.

With ten days before Christmas, Ciara didn't have time for a personal crisis when she had to save the world.

I did that on the cross, God whispered.

Ciara paused as the Lord pricked her heart for what she thought. "Lord, I know You're our Savior, so give me wisdom in my giving. In Jesus' name. Amen."

She did as God instructed in James 1:5: *If any of you lack wisdom, let him ask of God who gives it liberally to all without making ashamed for asking.*

Maybe Sterling was right about her shopping frenzy around Christmas. How could she set an example to the world who didn't know Christ? That hurt her to admit, but she didn't have time to repair a heartache now. Ciara would never go over budget again.

On Friday, she would begin to deliver gifts she had purchased and stockpiled in her basement.

The items had to be divvied up between some of her personal cases and those on the Help 100 Families list.

Case number fifty-eight's needs were too great for Ciara, and she was still going through her phone campaign, contacting dormant donors for contributions.

The odds seem to be stacked against this single mother of a baby girl. She wants to finish school but needs childcare. This mother doesn't have stable housing and sleeps at different places on a regular basis. She doesn't have transportation or a computer to seek permanent housing and employment. Her wish list is a job, a car, and a small room to rent.

"Lord, open a door that no man can shut, and supply this mother's needs according to Your riches." Ciara paused. When was the last time she'd prayed that prayer over families? For years, she had tried to be the heroine, and her disagreement with Sterling was proof she was losing the battle.

Closing her eyes, Ciara sighed. Was she that bad? Did she need an intervention?

If so, it would have to wait until next year. There was no time, especially when people needed help now.

There was case number sixty-nine. A mother was recovering from major hip surgery.

Not much money is left from her small monthly disability, which barely covers her medical bills and household expenses. Despite her situation, she needs help to send her son off to college, who is a straight-A student, with what he needs: bedding, clothes, and shoes would be a blessing.

A blessing. Ciara hummed a few chords of the old hymn "Make Me a Blessing." She was about to pray for this family when Terri raced into her office. "Run an updated donation report."

Startled, Ciara frowned. "Why? I did on Monday. Cases fifty-six through seventy were profiled."

"Run it again," Terri insisted, bobbing her head.

Ciara did. She stared, blinked, then stared again. "Five thousand and ten dollars," she stuttered. The donation came from Every Dime We Spend. Her eyes watered as she looked up at Terri.

Sterling's company, they seemed to whisper at the same time.

"What's up with the ten dollars?" Terri snickered.

"Don't know." Ciara refreshed her screen to make sure the amount hadn't vanished. Despite their second argument in days, Sterling gave a donation, but why didn't he go through her like he always did? She reached for her cell instead of the office line.

"Sterling, thank you for keeping your commitment, even though you're mad at me. Five thousand and ten dollars was a generous donation to Help 100 Families."

"Five thousand dollars?" he said, sounding surprised.

Amused by his act, Ciara chuckled. "Plus, the ten bucks."

"That wasn't me." His tone was tight.

"What do you mean?" Ciara panicked. "Oh no. What was the amount you actually gave?"

He was slow in answering. "Zero."

Her heart dropped.

"Let me get back to you." The call ended without Sterling's goodbye.

Taking a deep breath, Ciara had a sinking feeling there would be a refund. She dropped her head in her waiting hands. There really was a Grinch trying to steal Christmas.

Chapter Fifteen

Sterling was hot.

One suspect.

No, he didn't. Only two people were authorized to make donations on behalf of Every Dime We Spend. Sterling Price and Dray Blakely.

Lord, please keep my temper in check, Sterling prayed as he measured his steps from his office to Dray's. *Never accuse. Let the guilty party incriminate themselves,* he coaxed himself.

Sterling appeared in his business partner's doorway. His friend waved him in as he finished a call.

Folding his arms and leaning against the doorjamb, Sterling declined. "I just got a call from Ciara."

Dray's grin was so exaggerated that Sterling could count his teeth. "Yeah, I bet you did. I guess you're her hero again."

"And why is that?" Sterling approached the desk and took a seat.

Throwing up his arms, Dray grinned. "Listen, everybody is a winner. You may not want me to win a bet against Kenneth, but I know you won't deny your pretty lady friend help so that she won't have to work a Walmart job and—"

Sterling held up his hand. "Stop right there. Number one, you are too much in my business. Number two, she quit. Number three, I had planned to make one more donation on behalf of our company for one thousand dollars, and that would have been the budget I set for giving, not five thousand." He snarled. "What's up with the ten dollars?"

He chuckled. "Guess I've been watching too many reruns of *The Price Is Right*. The ten bucks could represent the difference of us winning. Anyway, I got your back, and if she's your damsel in distress, I rescued her on your behalf. *Thank you* would have been nice."

Rubbing the back of his head, Sterling got up and paced the office. "I can't fix this. Instead of making me look like a hero, you're forcing me to be the bad guy." He huffed.

"You're too serious, man." Dray shrugged and turned back to his keyboard.

"This company is successful because we're a team." Sterling pointed from himself to Dray. "We create expenditures and stick to the budget. This grandiose tax break you think we're getting under the guise of beating out Kenneth's contributions could mean we would have to put a freeze on hiring the additional staff we need."

"I don't think so. That contribution barely affects our cash flow." Dray was defiant.

What a mess. Christmas was not about going into debt for charity's sake.

"My—our—donation isn't going to shut this company down. Chill. One thing we—you—can't do is ask for it back." Smug, Dray folded his arms behind his head.

Sterling squinted at his friend, thinking about it in terms of ex-friend status. He pivoted on his heels, retraced his steps back to his office, and closed the door. Sterling flopped into his chair and closed his eyes.

He loved Ciara. Sterling froze in his thoughts. Then why was he mad at her? He exhaled.

What now? He began to pray. *"Lord, I repent of my behavior and thoughts. Help me not to be quick to judge Ciara for her giving heart, and Dray..."* He paused to think of how to describe his business partner. The only words that came to mind were Dray and his competitive spirit. *"Jesus, what should I do without hurting those who need the help?"*

By late afternoon, God still hadn't spoken, and Sterling's spirit was on high alert as he listened for the Lord's whispers or guidance from a Scripture.

Sterling couldn't talk to Ciara or Dray until he did, for fear of saying the wrong thing that would cause him to repent later.

"It's Christmastime, it's giving time, so all this shouldn't be happening." His frustration never dimmed.

A little past five o'clock, Sterling locked his office door. He was no closer on how to proceed. He hadn't been in the best mood since he'd left Ciara's the day before. In fact, his heart ached. In the brief time they had started dating, Sterling felt empty, not hearing her voice or giggles.

With loving kindness, I have drawn thee. God whispered a portion of Jeremiah 31:3.

Sterling froze mid-step toward his car. His spiritual senses took dominance, but the Lord said nothing more. As he continued to his vehicle, he almost slipped, not seeing the ice beneath his feet.

He chuckled to himself. God had kept him steady. Once behind the wheel, he detoured to his parents' home. His mother fed him, his sister hugged him, then he stretched out in the family room with his father.

"So, Dad, what would you do?" Sterling sought counsel after giving him a recap. "I get I'm not to be angry with Dray or Ciara, but I am for different reasons."

Thomas Price didn't interrupt as Sterling rambled on. Was he asleep with his eyes open?

Finally, he spoke. "I would do nothing. What's done is done. Son, Dray's heart was in the right place, although it wasn't necessarily the best way to go about it. As for Ciara, your mom and I like her—"

"Don't forget me," Briana shouted from the other room.

The men shook their heads, then Thomas continued. "I know you're not mad at her for accepting the money, but you've had a hang-up with women and money. I'm sure she didn't say it the way you heard it. She's good for you. Before she met you, you, my son, were already a sugar daddy for Help 100 Families."

"Sugar daddy?" Sterling laughed until his stomach hurt.

"Yep. I'm up with the latest slang. Son, take my advice. Apologize again and be happy."

"That's it?" Sterling eyed his dad. "Why does that seem to be your answer whenever I'm spilling my guts?"

"The Bible says love covers a multitude of faults. The footnote when it comes to women is apologizing first makes your life better." He grinned and pointed the remote at the flat screen.

Sterling's counseling session had ended.

WAS IT A SCAM?

Ciara didn't know what to think or do about the five-thou-sand-and-ten-dollar donation from Sterling's company yester-day to Help 100 Families.

Gnawing on her lips, Ciara wondered if the contribution should have been five hundred dollars or even ten. But Sterling said there was no donation.

Still not hearing from Sterling this morning, Ciara opened a ticket to the fraud department to investigate after she advised them of her concerns.

"Lord, please don't let it be a mistake," she whispered over and over. Those families could use that money. She refused to be in limbo for another day, so she called Sterling. This was no longer about their disagreement. This was about real people.

She braced herself for unfavorable news when he answered. "Hey."

"Hey." He was quiet.

That's all you have to say? "I guess the donation was an error and you want the money back." She held her breath and closed her eyes, waiting for him to confirm it.

"The money is real, Ciara. Dray made the donation, so he says, to clear the air between us, but he had another motive. He wanted to ensure our company would win a contribution com-petition."

"*Sooo,* we have to give the money back?" She swallowed.

"I can't do that to you. How can I justify taking money back from a worthy cause and maintain a good conscience?" He huffed.

Just because Sterling didn't ask for the money back now didn't mean he wouldn't.

Why did she feel bad keeping the money? It was a tug-of-war with her emotions. Guilt was winning. "Sterling, I know honesty between us lately hasn't been easy. I want there to still be an 'us.'"

"I'd have eventually said that." She imagined his smile as he continued, "How about dinner after work?"

Ciara pouted. "I'm working late tonight."

"Let me know when you're on your way home, and I'll bring dinner to you."

She smiled, knowing he would. A man who would brave the crowds at Walmart to make sure she ate was special.

"No, I won't stay too late, then I'll stop and get us something to eat, and you can meet me at my house. My treat."

"That gives me something to look forward to." After some air kisses over the phone, Sterling was gone.

"Lord, change the hearts of former donors and bring in new ones." There had to be a Plan C where she could convince companies to donate surpluses. She sighed. But even that wasn't enough. These single mothers needed transportation and safe daycare to work or go to school. To make that happen, she needed a Christmas miracle. Seventeen cases were profiled this weekend with thirty more families to go.

She reviewed the list of items she had shopped for out of her own pocket: electronics, including laptops, iPads, phones, and three televisions; sweaters; socks; blankets; and coats. Ciara prayed again, *Lord, multiply my meager gifts like Jesus performed with the fish and loaves. In Jesus' name Amen.*

Of all the families profiled, Ciara was concerned about Arlene Green. She had hinted a while back that she might put her children up for adoption, if something didn't change by Christmas. On paper, it would be best for the children, but emotionally, the grandmother and grandbabies would lose the connection. Ciara didn't know if the young mother was bluffing, and she didn't want to find out.

The other was case number fifty-eight. *A single mother of a baby girl, sleeping at different houses each night. That alone made Ciara shiver with safety concerns for the mother,*

Ciara silently prayed as Sterling's ringtone interrupted her.

"Please tell me you're on your way home." There was panic in Sterling's voice.

"No." She grinned. "It's okay if you can't wait to eat. You can—"

"Baby," he cut her off, "I'm not worried about food. Did you get the alerts on your phone about the winter weather advisory—five or more inches of snow are on the way. I sent my staff home early. Are you sure it's a good idea for you to work late?"

Ciara had ignored her texts. She gritted her teeth in uncertainty. "Oh no. Not good. I might like the winter, but driving in that much snow is not my favorite pastime. I'll wrap it up and get out the door within the next thirty minutes."

"Ciara, I'll be there in twenty-nine minutes to drive you home."

Her heart melted. She wanted to hold on to Sterling Price. There was no sense in arguing with him anymore about anything. "O-okay. Thank you." She was falling harder for him.

"See you soon. If you get stranded at work, I'll be there with you. Otherwise, I'm driving you home."

"What about you getting stranded?"

"Santa had Rudolph in fairy tales. I've got Jesus. Bye."

Chapter Sixteen

Sterling wasn't worried about himself being stranded. He was concerned about Ciara. To be prepared for anything, he took extra blankets, a shovel, salt and first aid items, then dashed out of the house.

He gripped the steering wheel while his wipers counterattacked the snow. He was losing the battle despite his wipers' best efforts. The thirty minutes stretched into forty-seven before he double-parked in front of Ciara's office.

The snow raged on, thicker flakes and faster as if to punish drivers. Sterling stepped out with his shovel and carved a path from the passenger side to the front door.

He expected Ciara to be ready and waiting.

No.

Sterling knocked on the door three times. He pounded more forcefully each time until she appeared.

"Sorry." Ciara was breathless and beautiful, but not ready. "I've been distracted. Two cases have me concerned..." she began, then waved her hand as she walked back to her office. "Never mind. I shouldn't talk about it anyway"

"Ciara..." He grabbed her hand and slowed her down. "Tell me why those cases are heavy on your heart. Leave out names or their case numbers to protect their privacy."

She nodded and inhaled. "Okay. Handouts help, but these ladies want jobs and to better themselves with education. Basic needs that are hard to meet without childcare." Her expression was fierce.

Sterling refrained from shutting down her computer and putting her coat on like a parent does his child, then carrying her in his arms to his Jeep. "Babe, I think we'd better hurry. You can finish telling me in the car."

"Right. Right." She collected her things.

Once they were strapped into his vehicle, Sterling concentrated on the road and listened to Ciara's pleas. "One family I know personally, and the other case, I can hear the woman's voice in my head. They want to work."

His mind shuffled possibilities. "Dray and I had planned to hire two or more people in the new year. Those positions are entry-level and could be remote since we're an internet-based company. They will start off as part-time, hopefully transition them into full-time by the second quarter."

"Because of the donations?" Her voice was low.

Sterling didn't want that to be her burden. "Partly. No telling what else is on his agenda." One glance was all it took for Sterling to see the moisture in her eyes.

"If the Lord makes a way out of this impossible situation, I'll consider them on a temp basis, if that would help." *Lord, only You can fix this.*

Out of the corner of his eye, Sterling saw her staring at him. "You would do that for me—I mean them?"

He chuckled. "You said it right the first time. For you and those families."

Ciara's phone rang. She smiled, then answered. "Hi, Daddy." She paused. "Yes, I'm on my way home... No, I'm not driving.

Sterling came to get me." She tapped speaker on the phone. "Okay, he can hear you."

"Sterling, thank you," he said, choking, "for making sure my little girl is safe."

Ciara rolled her eyes at the *little girl* term.

"You're welcome. I love Ciara, and I want her safe and happy." He chanced a quick glance at her before turning his attention back to the road.

"One more thing."

"Yes, sir?"

"Make sure *you* don't get stranded at her place."

Sterling nodded. "Never crossed my mind."

"We have to go, Daddy, so he can concentrate on the road." She disconnected and scrunched her nose. "Sorry."

"He's a protective father." Sterling maneuvered the slick spots. "I respect that but have no intentions of staying at your place."

Five miles from Ciara's house, Sterling's wipers were losing the battle with the layers of snow. He shifted his Jeep into 4x4.

"Do you think we'll make it?" She looked doubtful.

"Yes, in Jesus' name."

"Amen. I hope they have the streets cleared by Friday." The worry in Ciara's voice matched her frown once he glanced at her.

"What's happening on Friday?"

"I'm delivering the gifts to families."

He nodded. "Oh. Can I be your designated driver and carry some of those gifts?"

She tilted her head and studied him. "I'd like that. All I ask is that you respect the privacy of our families if any are recognizable. My family already knows the routine."

"Understood." For the next twenty minutes, they skated on unplowed streets. A few times, Ciara squeezed his hand. "What I don't understand is why social services doesn't do more to get the families what they need."

Ciara was quiet. She fumbled with her gloves. "Funding, backlog, politics, increase in cases. Take your pick. One act of kindness around Christmas could be life changing. Many of those gifts come from Help 100 Families."

Will my donations be life changing? Sterling wondered.

"For example, one family lost two sons to gangs. The teenagers thought selling drugs was their only option to earn money to take care of their families," Ciara paused. "One woman turned to prostitution to feed her child. Later, she was murdered. The struggle is real." She sniffed, and he reached for her hand.

Although Sterling had no say in giving her the five thousand and ten dollars, he was glad Dray did, and more importantly, Sterling didn't ask for it back.

They were quiet as Sterling's tires barreled against the snow. "You know what, I'll consider hiring those two women you mentioned."

"How?" The shock was on her face and in her voice.

"A business loan." Sterling smiled.

She smiled, then had a questioning expression. "Thank you for offering to do that, but can we back track?" Ciara waited for him to nod. "Did you mean what you told my father. I mean do you love me as a sister-in-Christ—"

"Sorry, I should have said that to you first. Both as a woman and as my sister-in-Christ. If a man remembers that, he'd never violate her. And I do love you, Ciara Summers.

"Wow, if I didn't love you before, I'd definitely be falling hard now." Ciara patted her chest as her eyes reflected the love he had for her. "I love you too."

He wanted to kiss her. Instead, his Jeep stole the moment when it plowed into a snow mound when he turned the corner. They were blocks away from Ciara's house.

"Oh, no." She gritted her teeth. "Now what?"

Sterling didn't answer as he climbed out and kicked the snow aside to get to his shovel and salt from the rear. It didn't take long for him to lose the battle against the elements. He opened her passenger door. "Grab your stuff and come on."

"What? Where are we going? My ankle boots are no match for all this snow." She hesitated.

"You trust me?"

"Yes." She did as he said. "And love you."

Sterling held his breath and stared into her eyes, then he smiled. Every time she said it felt new. "I love you more." Then he scooped her up in his arms. At first, she protested, then snuggled closer to his chest.

"Am I heavy?" She looked concerned as he locked his car and began the trek to her house.

"Yep." He chuckled.

"Hey, you're supposed to say, 'No, you're light as a feather' or 'I bench press whatever the heaviest weight' or something sweet."

"You are the sweetest thing to me. I'll carry you as long as God gives my arms strength."

One block—done. Two blocks—barely. The third and final block seemed never ending. He would have to add weights in the gym after this, for sure. Finally, he delivered her to her porch, then he released her.

Not as gently as he wanted.

"Thank you. Do you want to come in to get warm or something hot to drink?"

"No. I better try and make it home."

"Sterling, you could barely make it here."

"I was on foot and carrying a load."

"Oh, you've got jokes. Not funny." Her eyes pleaded with him to listen to reasoning. "How will you dig yourself out? Do you have enough gas?" She took a breath.

"Babe, I'm a man's man." God knew he didn't want Mr. Summers to suspect his emergency stay as a ploy for a passionate night. Nope. Wasn't going to happen. Plus, he wouldn't disrespect Ciara and subject her to rumors among her neighbors. "I'd better go."

Ciara pouted. "O-okay." She gave him a warm kiss. "Call me as soon as you make it home. Jesus, please watch over him and keep the man I love safe."

He drew in a deep breath and exhaled. "I like the sound of being your man as much as knowing you're the woman I love." Sterling pressed his cold lips against hers again, then took off.

As he tried to retrace his steps back to his vehicle, Sterling accepted there was no way he could make it home. He called Dray who didn't live far away. They may have had a disagreement, but at the end of the day, they had each other's back. "Hey, I need a favor."

"You got it."

"If I can make it to your house, can I crash for the night?"

"Done. You don't have to ask. Where are you? I'll come and help plow you out. Two shovels are better than one."

"Yes, they are, bro." Sterling grinned and gave him the intersection. "Thanks."

"That's what friends are for."

"No, that's what my brother is for." Sterling ended the call. His feet seemed to thaw as his heart warmed and he thought about the Scripture: *Be angry, but sin not.*

Tonight, he learned another life lesson: no misunderstanding or disagreement was worth losing a friend.

PEEKING OUT HER WINDOW from inside of her warm house, Ciara prayed for Sterling as the snowstorm sucked him in. "Lord, keep him from getting hyperthermia.

The poem about footprints in the sand came to mind where two sets became one, signifying Jesus carried the weight. Sterling had carried her. "Lord, please carry him."

Snuggled in a throw around her shoulders and sipping on hot chocolate, Ciara paced her living room, trying to build up her faith to trust God to take care of Sterling, the drivers on the road, the homeless out in the elements, homes without heat...

Three minutes felt like thirty minutes when not knowing about his well-being. Ciara called Sterling and got his voicemail. She tugged on her hair. Was his battery dead? Did he freeze to death, or maybe his phone had gotten lost in a mountain of snow.

"Hey, it's me. Are you okay? Please call me when you get this message."

Suddenly, she was too warm. Ciara removed the throw and dumped it on the sofa and peeped out the window again. The snow continued to fall as the what-ifs began to plague her. *Keep praying for faith,* she told herself.

Don't be anxious for nothing! Pray and submit to Me, and I'll hear your requests. God whispered Philippians 4:6.

Chastened, Ciara repented, then padded to the bathroom. Sterling's ringtone played. Bad timing. Her bladder couldn't wait any longer; neither could her heart. She raced toward her phone.

"You made it." She held her breath.

"Yep. I'm staying at Dray's."

Ciara exhaled. "Thank You, Jesus. Now I've got to go."

Chapter Seventeen

"New Year's Day is around the corner. Make it your resolution to pump more weighs at the gym." Dray laughed all night and still chuckled because Sterling had carried Ciara home. "I've got heating pads, bro."

With a steaming mug of coffee, Sterling forced an opening in Dray's blinds. The plow trucks had made minimum inroads on the streets, but at least it had stopped snowing.

"I'm cool. My football back injury didn't flare up once." Sterling had declined them last night and now. He couldn't remember the last time he used heating pads. With his phone charged, he called to check in on Ciara, who was working from home.

An hour later, he and Dray were doing the same until Dray's street was clear enough for Sterling to drive to his house. The roads still weren't in the best condition, but he made it.

That evening, Ciara came up with an idea about a virtual dinner over Zoom.

"I'm not feeling it. I can't hold your hand, get lost in those dazzling eyes and kiss you when the mood hits me."

"Promises, promises, promises. You can make good when we're together. Until that romantic moment, let's see what's in our freezer, and I'll email you a Zoom link. Bye."

And she was gone, but the happiness in her voice lingered, so he did as she requested. Besides TV dinners, he had a chicken, then he spied hamburger patties. He grabbed two, then his lap-top.

"Let the cookout begin." He grinned as he flipped a frozen patty, which missed the skillet.

Ciara laughed until her eyes teared. Sterling couldn't help himself and laughed too.

His woman showed off with a chicken and shrimp stir-fry. Sterling's senses played tricks on him, and he thought he could smell it. Turned out, he burned his burger, mesmerized by her every movement.

When it was time to eat, he blessed their food. "I guess this isn't too bad." He smacked his lips. "Hopefully, the streets are cleared enough tomorrow morning, so I can take you to get your car and have a date night."

She shook her head. "Snow or rain isn't going to stop me from my annual Christmas gifts drop-off, remember?"

He didn't.

"On that note, I need to finish wrapping gifts."

A mischievous plot came to Sterling's mind. "I can help you wrap from afar."

"Ha! Now, you're silly, but I love you."

"I love you too." He folded his arms on his home desk. "I'll play Christmas music to serenade us and supervise your wrap-ping skills."

"You're really getting into this, but I'm the wrapping queen." She stuck out her tongue. "Let me get my stuff set up and call you back."

The snow had stopped. Some streets were cleared. Sterling shut down his computer and grabbed his keys. He was off to another adventure. At least, this time, he wouldn't have to carry his woman. His back thanked him.

Chapter Eighteen

Eight days before Christmas, Ciara stood in her doorway watching Sterling manhandle his Jeep to her partially visible curb. The streets were passable, but the sideways had vanished in plain sight.

If the forecasters were right about a warmup, the streets would be in better conditions for Ciara to deliver gifts later after work.

When he stepped on her porch, Sterling towered over her, then he reached for her laptop. "Good morning, my love." He grinned as he inhaled the chilly air. "I like saying that."

"I like hearing it from you." Ciara locked her door. Sterling kept her steady on the walkway, then opened the passenger door.

They strapped their seatbelts at the same time after he slid behind the wheel. Ciara smiled. "You're spoiling me. Thank you." She leaned closer, and he met her for a kiss. "I thought I was okay not being in a relationship, but you've shown me the perks I've been missing. You love Jesus, you love me, and you respect me. What more could I ask for?"

A ring, her heart shouted. Ciara ignored the thought. She was in a happy place and content.

"Woman, I'm trying not to blush." Sterling checked the rearview mirror and skated his vehicle out onto the street.

The ride to her job was smooth, but careful. They passed Sterling's office in Mid-town on the way to her downtown office. When they arrived at her building, Sterling parked.

Ciara frowned. "You don't have to escort me inside. The sidewalks have been shoveled and salted. I won't slip."

He held out his hand. "I want your keys to make sure your car will start."

She handed the over without further protest, then continued inside to her office. At her desk, Ciara's mind shifted from swooning over Sterling to reviewing the fate of families—the "haves" and the "have nots" who received donations. All the contributions received to date weren't spread across the board equally.

She logged into her program to scan cases seventy-one through ninety, which would be profiled over the weekend.

Ciara looked up to see Sterling in her doorway. She waved him in.

"Your car starts, but you only have a half tank of gas." He *tsk*ed. "Miss Summers, I need you to keep your tank full in the winter—really all the time. You could have gotten stranded and ran out of gas the other night."

Amused, Ciara folded her arms on her desk. He sounded like her father. It was endearing and loving.

"If you don't want to fill your car up, I'll do it every Sunday evening."

Ciara wiggled her finger for him to come closer, so he leaned across her desk. She whispered, "I love you." The kiss was brief, but it made him grin.

"Yeah. That will hold me until later." He backed away without taking his eyes off hers. "What time do you start with your gift drop-offs?"

"Four. I'm leaving here at three."

"Okay." He bobbed his head. "I'll take care of some things at the office, then meet you at your house before four."

"Sterling, thank you for being in my life." She choked getting the words out. "You are my Christmas gift."

"Mine too. I guess Every Dime We Spend's donation was worth it for our paths to cross." He winked and left her office.

STERLING DIDN'T KNOW what he signed up for when he parked in front of Ciara's house. Two other cars were there. Was this her caravan? He grunted and shook his head. "My woman."

He stepped out and hiked up the stairs to her porch. Her father was inside gathering gifts Sterling hadn't seen the other night. Larry Summers walked passed him, huffing.

Sterling didn't waste time loading up. He noticed the other vehicles had gifts stacked high. He could only imagine their trunks. He smirked.

"Let's go, people," Mr. Summers said to his wife, daughters, son-in-law, and grandchildren.

With Ciara riding with him, Sterling led the way. "What's the address of the first stop?"

He programmed the location and was surprised the family wasn't far from his office.

Because the side street wasn't well plowed, Sterling doubled park and had to maneuver the slippery sidewalks with a large flat screen. "These are expensive gifts."

"But I got them at bargain prices."

"Yes, a night to remember that changed my life." Sterling winked, then frowned. "I–I'm not judging, baby, but most of the cases I've read asked for practical gifts."

"A television is practical. So is a cell phone, iPad, and other electronics," Ciara snapped. "Sorry, it's just a sore spot for me. You're not the first person to make that statement. I know how kind, generous and loving you are. Forgive me?"

How could he say no to her beautiful, misty eyes? "And forgive me. Now, let's do it and make somebody happy." He grinned as a peace offering.

Ciara kept her tone soft as Sterling walked by her side. "Poverty doesn't mean that a person can't have something extra, besides the basics. And you know I do extra."

"Yes, I do, and love you for it." Sterling had come to respect her passion.

The drop-offs seemed never-ending. He didn't complain doing the heavy lifting under Mr. Summers' watchful eye until all the gifts were gone from his car. Then her parents and Amber, who was riding with them, said their goodbyes.

It was eight o'clock when Sterling and Jessica's vehicles turned on an otherwise dark street except for the Christmas lights. Some spots had become slippery when the sun went down.

Ciara stepped out and signaled for Justin's son and daughter, who were dressed as angels, to come. They were excited to deliver goodies to other children.

Sterling brought up the rear with more electronics as Ciara rang the bell.

An older woman, who reminded him of his late grandmother, pushed the curtains aside and peeked out the window. Blinking lights made her face glow.

She opened the door wide, clutching her collar tight. "It's good to see you, Ciara."

"And you too, Mrs. Green."

The woman smiled as she glanced at the children. "And who do we have here, your helpers?"

Ciara nodded as Arlene appeared with her children. "Yep. My niece and nephew are God's little angels. They wrapped your grandbaby's gifts themselves."

Rocking from side to side, Justin Jr. and Dina grinned and displayed their presents out of their bags for the little ones.

"Arlene, I've got something for you too." She took a laptop from an oversized tote. "You can search for jobs."

Ciara smiled, but Arlene sighed. "Thanks, but I don't have childcare, and my mother can't keep up with them. Hope has run out."

Sterling had stayed on the sidelines as much as possible to respect the families' privacy all evening, but he couldn't bear to hear another dejected single mother who couldn't do better because of childcare. Their hopelessness was creating a wound in his heart. Was this one of the cases that had Ciara concerned?

He whispered the question in her ear, and Ciara nodded before Sterling cleared his throat. "I'm Sterling Price, co-founder of Every Dime We Spend, an Internet-based company. If you can pass a background check, I can offer you employment—part time for now. You can work from home, and we'll even assist you with college classes."

Arlene blinked, then looked from Sterling to Ciara. She was speechless. "Really? But I don't see how I can be productive with my little ones."

"We'll work out something." Sterling nodded, slipped a business card out of his wallet, and handed it to Arlene.

One tear fell from Ciara's eyes, followed by another. Soon, Ciara, Mrs. Green and Arlene had Sterling in a bear hug, sobbing. The children mimicked the adults. Soon, their tears manifested into praise as their hands lifted in the air and their feet patted the floor in a toddler's dance.

The anointing fell on Ciara. "Do you mind us praying?"

They consented, and Ciara asked Sterling to lead the prayer.

He bowed his head. "Father God, in the name of Jesus, we come boldly to Your throne of grace where we can receive mercy and forgiveness of our sins. Lord, we know You can do exceedingly, abundantly above all we can ask or think, so I'm asking for blessings for this family and the hundreds of others I haven't seen. Encourage their souls and supply all their needs, according to your endless riches in glory. In Jesus' name. Amen."

Arlene's children shouted, "Amen."

Minutes later, Ciara and her crew waved good night.

Inside his vehicle, Sterling had an unexplainable joy rooted within his spirit. "If this is the norm of God showing up and showing out, put me down for next year, if the Lord wills."

"Amen. If the Lord wills." Ciara smiled with a glow to her face. The prayer had done that.

"All evening, I've seen a taste of what you see and the hope and joy your gifts bring. I believe God will fill in the gap. Thank you for letting me tag along."

As they finished their two final deliveries, Sterling couldn't stop grinning. *This has been the best Christmas season ever.*

Chapter Nineteen

"This is Christmas," Ciara's pastor began his sermon. "You don't need a tree, lights, and presents to celebrate. All you need is a Savior, and the real celebration begins from within your soul and spills out."

Exchanging knowing glances, Sterling squeezed Ciara's hand.

Pastor Kent continued, "That should be our motivation to give gifts, because there's not enough room under the largest tree to hold the gifts Christ gave to men, and there are many of them mentioned in the Bible." The pastor scanned his notes and shared passages.

The inspiring message lined up with a sermon Sterling's own pastor had preached years ago.

"To celebrate a person's birthday, we're supposed to give them gifts, not to everybody else, but them. Keep that in mind when you're gift shopping. If you spend a hundred dollars on your wife—and it's Christ's birthday—make sure you give Him at least an offering of a hundred and one dollars."

That point stayed with the Prices and caused them to temper their spending and remain debt free during the holidays.

Sterling kept that in mind when he shopped online for the perfect gift for Ciara.

Pastor Kent pulled him back. "So today, don't be disheartened." He closed his Bible. "It's not about what you didn't get, rejoice for what you did receive—God's gifts bestowed on your soul, and the blessings ahead, if you follow Jesus, according to His will."

The invitation for salvation was given, and two parents with a teenager responded, wanting to give Jesus themselves as presents. They were baptized in water and in the Holy Ghost, in Jesus' name.

The church was in a celebratory mood as the pastor gave the benediction. Sterling and Ciara, along with others, were rejoicing as they left the service.

Once they were in his vehicle, he faced Ciara. "Ready? Now, you're sure your parents are okay with you spending most of the day with my family?"

Ciara smiled. "Yes. Daddy told me last night he's been waiting to share me with a special someone, and that someone is you."

"Wait. What? He said that" — he patted his chest— "about me?"

She nodded and snickered. "Like my brother-in-law won my father over with his secret barbecue sauce, you scored the winning point when you made sure I got home safe during the snowstorm." The love in her eyes was all that mattered to Sterling.

"And I would do it again." He winked. Maybe he should invest in a snowmobile for next time. Sterling intertwined his fingers through hers and drove off a happy man. God had given him an early Christmas gift, and he was grateful and whispered his thanks.

Sterling gave Ciara the impression they were heading to his parents' house. They were, but first he wanted some one-on-one time for them to celebrate Christmas alone.

When she realized they were driving toward South St. Louis County, Ciara faced him and squinted. "Where are we going? I thought you said your parents lived in Creve Coeur."

"They do." He smirked. "We're almost there. Be patient, beautiful."

Surprisingly, Ciara compiled, squeezing his hand and taking in the sights out the window. Ten minutes later, he turned on Sappington Road into Laumier Park, known for more than sixty outdoor sculptures.

He parked. Remnants of snow were on the sidewalk. They wouldn't walk far.

"What are we doing here?" Ciara asked when he opened her passenger door to help her out.

"I wanted to take a few minutes by ourselves before I share you with my family. Plus, I want to give you your present. I thought you would appreciate the outdoors setting."

"That's sweet. I know you're shivering," she teased.

"I won't be here long." Sterling took her hand and started toward the Museum Circle exhibits. When they came to the Tulips sculpture, he stopped.

"We have to come back here in the spring, summer and fall—all seasons." He grinned and exhaled the chilled air. If she didn't pick up his clues, Ciara would find out that he wanted to make their relationship last. He reached into his coat pocket and pulled out two boxes.

"*Awww.* You leave me speechless." Her eyes brighten, and she accepted them with a sweet thank you and the sweetest kiss. Then she ripped the gift paper back and removed the lid. "A charm bracelet. Wow. I haven't worn one in years. This is beautiful."

Sterling lifted it from its cotton cushion, opened the latch, and wrapped it around her small wrist. "It's a diamond heart charm bracelet in sterling silver instead of gold. It had to be sterling silver."

"Of course." She scrunched her nose in a tease, then fingered the two heart-shaped charms and... "an ice skate." Her smile widened and she rewarded him with more smooches.

"I should have brought more gifts because you're keeping my lips warm. I got the idea to add them when I saw a bracelet with sports charms, so I customized it to remind you—"

"Of our skate date. I'll never forget that day—never. The hearts are perfect. Thank you." She sealed another kiss to his lips.

The other box held mittens. "For your next stakeout."

Ciara's smile turned into a frown. "These are so thoughtful. My gift pales to yours."

He wrapped her in a hug. "Christmas isn't about a competition. Gifts aren't limited to Christmas."

"Right." Ciara cheered up and reached into her purse. She also had two small boxes.

Sterling choked. He couldn't remember the last time a lady friend bought him a gift. He accepted them in reverence. "Thank you, baby."

As he unwrapped them, Ciara explained, "Since you're always polished when I see you in a suit or casual, I got you an accessory for your suit. It's a monogrammed lapel pin and cuff links."

He chuckled. He would wear them with pride. "I'll be a trendsetter and wear it on sweaters, too, since my lady gave it to me. Maybe, my pants pockets."

Ciara laughed. "Okay, you're doing too much. I'm glad you like it. I couldn't resist the cufflink and stud set."

They were black onyx. His woman had good taste. "And I can't resist you." This time, he warmed her lips.

THE CHRISTMAS CHEER continued for Ciara at the Prices. Their smiles mirrored Sterling's as they welcomed her. Their visit to Laumeier Park and his gifts touched her deeply. Sterling wasn't a creature of cold weather, but he had chosen an outdoor landmark for her. He had no idea he had sparked a tit-for-tat emotion within her. She would be on the lookout for more thoughtful gifts to shower him with.

The Prices made gift opening a major production. "This gift card is for you." Mrs. Price smiled at Ciara before she opened the envelope. "Sterling tells me how selfless you are with others. Promise me you'll pamper yourself with this."

Sterling wrapped his arm around Ciara's shoulders and squeezed. He didn't seem surprised that each family member had gotten her something.

Touched by their kindness, Ciara sniffed. "I will. Thank you so much."

"You're welcome, dear." Mrs. Price's eyes twinkled.

"Briana and I decided to go in together." Danielle, his sister from Chicago, handed over a flat, square package.

"No telling what my two younger sisters have masterminded," Sterling joked, and his sisters playfully punched him in both arms, and he feigned injury. Everyone laughed.

"Thank you." Ciara removed the packaging and sucked in her breath. She fingered the sketch of her and Sterling. "This is priceless—no pun intended."

His mother laughed. "It's okay. We hear that pun all the time."

Briana explained, "We took individual pictures from your social media accounts and had them sketched together. We did it a week after you two met. I'm glad you didn't break up, then we would've had to pitch the gift."

"That wasn't going to happen." Sterling grunted as everyone else laughed.

Ciara couldn't stop looking at it. Two separate photos, yet the pose blended perfectly.

Mr. Price cleared his throat to get her attention. "I left the shopping to the ladies. In your name, I donated to Help 100 Families."

Ciara squealed as a tear fell. She choked as she tried to speak. Sterling squeezed her tight.

"Thank you all. I'm overwhelmed with your kindness." Ciara took a deep breath and exhaled. "I'm honestly speechless."

His mother patted her hand. "Don't be. From what our son says, you always put others before you. That's the type of woman my son needs. We want to keep you around a long time."

Ciara blushed, then looked at Sterling. "I want the same thing."

"Now, our tradition is to play a game. Your choice." His father pointed to the stack of board games. "Brace for a long night."

Chapter Twenty

After Christmas...

The week was theirs, free of distractions or demands. Sterling and Ciara were enjoying their Christmas vacation together. This was the third day in a row they had tried a new place for breakfast.

Sterling couldn't wait to celebrate the New Year with Ciara and create a romantic Valentine's Day she would never forget.

During the summer, the possibilities were endless—barbecues, ball games, and activities he had yet to imagine. Then, if the Lord wills, they could close out the year with their one-year anniversary.

Yeah, Sterling was thinking long term with Ciara. Gazing into her drugging brown eyes made him want a family. A wife. Children. The complete package.

Sterling blinked, not realizing Ciara had been talking to him.

"I said, you're a brave man to want to go shopping with me for after Christmas bargains." She lifted a brow in a challenge.

"I ain't scared. We're in this together. I don't ever want to see that heavy weight on my woman's shoulders again."

Reaching across the table at First Watch, Sterling played with her fingers. "Why wait until Christmas to bless these families? I can rent a space and have the community and other benefactors bring new and slightly used items for the needy year-round."

Ciara tilted her head, considering his idea. "Like a Goodwill, but free. I love it!" Her eyes widened with excitement. She scrambled to her feet and scooped up her hat, coat, and mittens. He did the same as she laughed. "It's never too early to start bargain hunting, so what are we waiting for? Let's go."

Good thing he had paid their tab. Linking hands, Sterling allowed Ciara to tug him to toward the door, forcing him to pick up his pace.

At his Jeep, he opened her door. "I understand why you didn't tell me the reason behind your shopping craze. What you do in secret, God rewards openly. I get it."

"Thank you for understanding." She lowered her lashes, then brushed her lips against his before she slid into her passenger seat.

Sterling got behind the wheel and started the engine. He thought about Dray. There was nothing covert about his intentions. "I also was reminded that God uses anyone to bless others. Dray gets the credit for adding that ten dollars with the five thousand for Every Dime We Spend to win bragging rights. Each family in Help 100 Families will get five hundred dollars on top of whatever else they received, courtesy of KenDixon Logistics. You should get their donation within a week."

Ciara shook her head. She seemed in awe. "Blessings seem to follow you, Mr. Price, and I'm glad I'm on the receiving end. Sounds like the Mighty Six are impressive Black men, and I'm proud of all your accomplishments."

Sterling accepted the accolades with humility as he rolled to a stop at a red light. He was startled when Ciara leaned over and wrapped her arms around his neck in almost a chokehold. She peppered kisses over his face, leaving evidence with her lipstick. "Thank You, God. Thank you, Dray, and thank you, Sterling, for coming into my life."

Laughing, Sterling indulged her. Yes, their love story would be an adventure, and he couldn't wait to experience each chapter with Ciara.

BOOKCLUB DISCUSSIONS

1. The 100NeediestCases.org is a real Christmas program in St. Louis and inspired me to write this story. What holiday programs does your city have to help those in need?
2. Although Every Dime We Spend is a fictional company, what can you do to support black and minority businesses?
3. What ways can you help families in need year-round?
4. Discuss your feelings about Dray's competitive nature in giving.
5. What was your favorite scene for *Waiting for Christmas*?
6. What spiritual message did you receive from the story?

Thanks so much for reading. Please consider any of the followings:

- Post a review on social platforms, so others will find *Waiting for Christmas*
- Rate it on Goodreads
- Recommend it on BookBub
- Mention *Waiting for Christmas* to friends and book clubs.

By the way, I hope you like the cover. My son was the cover model.

About the Author

Pat Simmons is a multi-published Christian romance author with more than thirty-five titles. She is a self-proclaimed genealogy sleuth who is passionate about researching her ancestors, then casting them in starring roles in her novels. She is a four-time recipient of the Romance Slam Jam Emma Rodgers Award for Best Inspirational Romance: *Still Guilty*, *Crowning Glory*, *The Confession*, and *Christmas Dinner*.

Pat's first inspirational women's fiction, *Lean on Me*, with Sourcebooks, was the February/March Together We Read Digital Book Club pick for the national library system. *Here for You* and *Stand by Me* are also part of the Family is Forever series. Her holiday indie release, *Christmas Dinner won RSJ 2021 Best Book of the Year* and *Best Inspirational Romance*. *Christmas Dinner* and *Here for You* were featured in *Woman's World*, a national magazine. *Here for You* was also listed in the "7 Great Reads That Help to Keep the Faith" by Sisters From AARP. She contributed an article, "I'm Listening" in the *Chicken Soup for the Soul: I'm Speaking Now* (2021).

Pat describes the evidence of the gift of the Holy Ghost as a life-altering experience. She has been a featured speaker and workshop presenter at various venues across the country. Pat has converted her sofa-strapped sports fanatical husband into an amateur travel agent, untrained bodyguard, GPS-guided chauffeur, and administrative assistant who is constantly on probation. They have a son and a daughter. Pat holds a B.S. in mass communications from Emerson College in Boston, Massachusetts and worked in various positions in radio, television, and print media for more than twenty years. She oversaw the media publicity for the annual RT Booklovers Conventions for fourteen years. Visit her at www.patsimmons.net.

Other Christian Titles

The Jamieson Legacy series:
    Book 1: *Guilty of Love*
Book 2: *Not Guilty of Love*
Book 3: *Still Guilty*
Book 4: *The Acquittal*
Book 5: *Guilty by Association*
Book 6: *The Guilt Trip*
Book 7: *Free from Guilt*
Book 8: *The Confession*
Book 9: *The Guilty Generation*
Book 10: *Queen's Surrender (To a Higher Calling)*
The Carmen Sisters series:
Book 1: *No Easy Catch*
Book 2: *In Defense of Love*
Book 3: *Driven to Be Loved*
Book 4: *Redeeming Heart*
Love at the Crossroads series:
Book 1: *Stopping Traffic*
Book 2: *A Baby for Christmas*
Book 3: *The Keepsake*
Book 4: *What God Has for Me*
Book 5: *Every Woman Needs a Praying Man*
Making Love Work Anthology
Book 1: *Love at Work*

Book 2: *Words of Love*

Book 3: *A Mother's Love*

<u>Restore My Soul series:</u>

Book 1: *Crowning Glory*

Book 2: *Jet: The Back Story*

Book 3: *Love Led by the Spirit*

<u>Family is Forever series:</u>

Book 1: *Lean on Me*

Book 2: *Here for You*

Book 3: *Stand by Me*

<u>God's Gifts series:</u>

Book1: *Couple by Christmas*

Book 2: *Prayers Answered by Christmas*

<u>Perfect Chance at Love series:</u>

Book 1: *Love by Delivery*

Book 2: *Late Summer Love*

<u>Single titles</u>

Talk to Me

Her Dress (novella)

Christmas Dinner

Christmas Greetings

Waiting for Christmas

Taye's Gift

<u>Anderson Brothers series:</u>

Book 1: *Love for the Holidays (Three novellas): A Christian Christmas, A Christian Easter, and A Christian Father's Day*

Book 2: *A Woman After David's Heart (Valentine's Day)*

Book 3: *A Noelle for Nathan (Book 3 of the Andersen Brothers)*

In *Love by Delivery*, Senior Accounts Manager Dominique Hayes has it all: money, a car, and a condo. Well, almost. She's starting to believe love has passed her by. One thing for sure, she can't hurry God, so she continues to wait while losing hope that a special Godly man will ever make his appearance. Package Courier Ashton Taylor knows a man who finds a wife finds a good thing. The only thing standing in his way of finding the right woman is his long work hours. Or maybe not. A chance meeting changes everything. When love finally comes knocking, will Dominique open the door and accept Ashton's special delivery?

In *Late Summer Love*, it takes strategies to win a war, but prayer and spiritual intervention are needed to win a godly woman's heart. God has been calling out to Blake Cross ever since Blake was deployed in Iraq and he took his safety for granted. Now, back on American soil, Blake still won't surrender his soul—until he meets Paige Blake during a family reunion. When the Lord gives Blake an ultimatum, is Blake listening, and is he finally ready to learn what it takes to be a godly man fit for a godly woman?

In *Crowning Glory*, Cinderella had a prince; Karyn Wallace has a King. While Karyn served four years in prison for an unthinkable crime, she embraced salvation through Crowns for Christ outreach ministry. After her release, Karyn stays strong and confident, despite the stigma society places on ex-offenders. Since Christ strengthens the underdog, Karyn refuses to sway away from the scripture, "He who the Son has set free is free indeed." Levi Tolliver, for the most part, is a practicing Christian. One contradiction is he doesn't believe in turning the other cheek. He's steadfast there is a price to pay for every sin committed, especially after the untimely death of his wife during a robbery. Then Karyn enters Levi's life. He is enthralled not only with her beauty, but her sweet spirit until he learns about her incarceration. If Levi can accept that Christ paid Karyn's debt in full, then a treasure awaits him. This is a powerful tale and reminds readers of the permanency of redemption.

Jet: The Back Story to Love Led By the Spirit, to say Jesetta "Jet" Hutchens has issues is an understatement. In Crowning Glory, Book 1 of the Restoring My Soul series, she releases a firestorm of anger with an unforgiving heart. But every hurting soul has a history. In Jet: The Back Story to Love Led by the

Spirit, Jet doesn't know how to cope with the loss of her younger sister, Diane. But God sets her on the road to a spiritual recovery. To make sure she doesn't get lost, Jesus sends the handsome and single Minister Rossi Tolliver to be her guide. Psalm 147:3 says Jesus can heal the brokenhearted and bind up their wounds. That sets the stage for Love Led by the Spirit.

In *Love Led By the Spirit*, Minister Rossi Tolliver is ready to settle down. Besides the outwardly attraction, he desires a woman who is sweet, humble, and loves church folks. Sounds simple enough on paper, but when he gets off his knees, praying for that special someone to come into his life, God opens his eyes to the woman who has been there all along. There is only a slight problem. Love is the farthest thing from Jesetta "Jet" Hutchens' mind. But Rossi, the man and the minister, is hard to resist. Is Jet ready to allow the Holy Spirit to lead her to love?

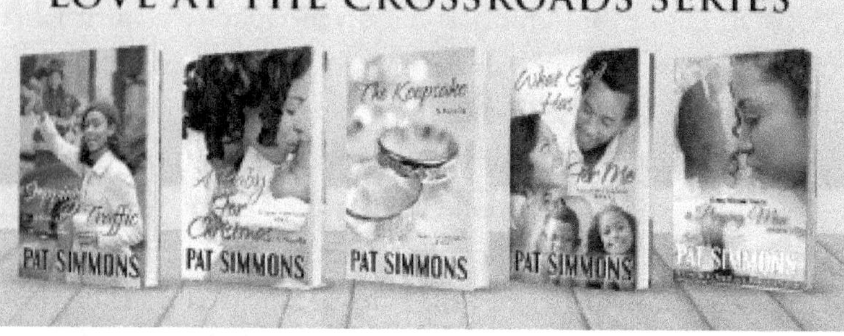

LOVE AT THE CROSSROADS SERIES

In *Stopping Traffic*, Book 1, Candace Clark has a phobia about crossing the street, and for good reason. As fate would have it, her daughter's principal assigns her to crossing guard duties as part of the school's Parent Participation program. With no choice in the matter, Candace begrudgingly accepts her stop sign and safety vest, then reports to her designated crosswalk. Once Candace is determined to overcome her fears, God opens the door for a blessing, and Royce Kavanaugh enters her life, a firefighter built to rescue any damsel in distress. When a spark of attraction ignites, Candace and Royce soon discover there's more than one way to stop traffic.

In *A Baby For Christmas*, Book 2, yes, diamonds are a girl's best friend, but in Solae Wyatt-Palmer's case, she desires something more valuable. Captain Hershel Kavanaugh is a divorcee and the father of two adorable little boys. Solae has never been married and longs to be a mother. Although Hershel showers her with expensive gifts, his hesitation about proposing causes Solae to walk and never look back. As the holidays approach, Hershel must convince Solae that she has everything he could ever want for Christmas.

In *The Keepsake*, Book 3, Until death us do part...or until Desiree walks away. Desiree "Desi" Bishop is devastated when she finds evidence of her husband's affair. God knew she didn't get married only to one day stand before a judge and file for a divorce. But Desi wants out no matter how much her heart says to forgive Michael. That isn't easier said than done. She sees God's one acceptable reason for a divorce as the only opt-out clause in her marriage. Michael Bishop is a repenting man who loves his wife of three years. If only...he had paid attention to the red flags God sent to keep him from falling into the devil's snares. But Michael didn't and he had fallen. Although God had forgiven him instantly when he repented, Desi's forgiveness is moving as a snail's pace. In the end, after all the tears have been shed and forgiveness granted and received, the couple learns that some marriages are worth keeping

In *What God Has For Me*, Book 4, Halcyon Holland is leaving her live-in boyfriend, taking their daughter and the baby in her belly with her. She's tired of waiting for the ring, so she buys herself one. When her ex doesn't reconcile their relationship, Halcyon begins to second-guess whether she compromised her chance for a happily ever after. After all, what man in his right mind would want to deal with the community stigma of 'baby mama drama?' But Zachary Bishop has had his eye on Halcyon since the first time he saw her. Without a ring on her finger, Zachary prays that she will come to her senses and not only leave Scott, but come back to God. What one man doesn't cherish; Zach is ready to treasure. Not deterred by Halcyon's broken spirit, Zachary is on a mission to offer her a second chance at love that she can't refuse. And as far as her adorable children are concerned, Zachary's love is unconditional for a ready-made family. Halcyon will soon learn that her past circumstances won't hinder the Lord's blessings, because what God has for her, is for her...and him...and the children.

In *Every Woman Needs a Praying Man*, Book 5, first impressions can make or break a business deal and they could be a relationship buster, but an ill-timed panic attack draws two strangers together. Unlike firefighters who run into danger, instincts tell businessman Tyson Graham to head the other way as fast as he can when he meets a certain damsel in distress. Days later, the same woman struts through his door for a job interview. Monica Wyatt might possess the outwardly beauty and the brains on paper, but Tyson doesn't trust her to work for his firm, or maybe he doesn't trust his heart around her.

In *A Christian Christmas*, Book 1, Christian's Christmas will never be the same for Joy Knight if Christian Andersen has his way. Not to be confused with a secret Santa, Christian and his family are busier than Santa's elves making sure the Lord's blessings are distributed to those less fortunate by Christmas day. Joy is playing the hand that life dealt her, rearing four children in a home that is on the brink of foreclosure. She's not looking for a handout, but when Christian rescues her in the checkout line; her niece thinks Christian is an angel. Joy thinks he's just another man who will eventually leave, disappointing her and the children. Although Christian is a servant of the Lord, he is a flesh and blood man and all he wants for Christmas is Joy Knight. Can time spent with Christian turn Joy's attention from her financial woes to the real meaning of Christmas—and true love?

In *A Christian Easter*, how to celebrate Easter becomes a balancing act for Christian and Joy Andersen and their four children. Chocolate bunnies, colorful stuffed baskets and flashy fashion shows are their competition. Despite the enticements, Christian refuses to succumb without a fight. And it becomes a tug of war when his recently adopted ten-year-old daughter, Bethani, wants to participate in her friend's Easter tradition.

Christian hopes he has instilled Proverbs 22:6, into the children's heart in the short time of being their dad.

In *A Christian Father's Day*, three fathers, one Father's Day and four children. Will the real dad, please stand up? It's never too late to be a father—or is it? Christian Andersen was looking forward to spending his first Father's Day with his adopted children—-all four of them. But Father's Day becomes more complicated than Christian, or Joy ever imagined. Christian finds himself faced with living up to his name when things don't go his way to enjoy an idyllic once a year celebration. But he depends on God to guide him through the journey.

(All three of Christian's individual stories are in the Love for the Holidays)

In *A Woman After David's Heart*, Book 2, David Andersen doesn't have a problem indulging in Valentine's Day, per se, but not on a first date. Considering it was the love fest of the year, he didn't want a woman to get any ideas that a wedding ring was forthcoming before he got a chance to know her. He has no choice but to wait until the whole Valentine's Day hoopla was over, then he would make his move on a sister in his church that caught his eyes. For the past two years and counting, Valerie Hart hasn't been the recipient of a romantic Valentine's Day dinner invitation. To fill the void, Valerie keeps herself busy with God's business, hoping the Lord will send her perfect mate soon. Unfortunately, with no prospects in sight, it looks like that won't happen again this year. A Woman After David's Heart is a Valentine romance novella that can be enjoyed with or without a box of chocolates.

In *A Noelle for Nathan*, Book 3, is a story of kindness, self-lessness, and falling in love during the Christmas season. Andersen Investors & Consultants, LLC, CFO Nathan Andersen (A Christian Christmas) isn't looking for attention when he buys a homeless man a meal, but grade schoolteacher Noelle Foster is watching his every move with admiration. His generosity makes him a man after her own heart. While donors give more to children and families in need around the holiday season, Noelle Foster believes in giving year-round after seeing many of her students struggle with hunger and finding a warm bed at night. At a second-chance meeting, sparks fly when Noelle and Nathan share a kindred spirit with their passion to help those less fortunate. Whether they're doing charity work or attending Christmas parties, the couple becomes inseparable. Although Noelle and Nathan exchange gifts, the biggest present is the one from Christ.

This series can be read in any order.

In *A Mother's Love*, to Jillian Carter, it's bad when her own daughter beats her to the altar. She became a teenage mother when she confused love for lust one summer. Despite the sins of her past, Jesus forgave her and blessed her to be the best Christian example for Shana. Jillian is not looking forward to becoming an empty nester at thirty-nine. The adage, she's not losing a daughter, but gaining a son-in-law is not comforting as she braces for a lonely life ahead. What she doesn't expect is for two men to vie for her affections: Shana's biological father who breezes back into their lives as a redeemed man and practicing Christian. Not only is Alex still goof looking, but he's willing to right the wrong he's done in the past. Not if Dr. Dexter Harris has anything to say about it. The widower father of the groom has set his sights on Jillian and he's willing to pull out all the stops to woo her. Now the choice is hers. Who will be the next mother's love?

In *Love at Work*, how do two people go undercover to hide an office romance in a busy television newsroom? In plain sight, of course. Desiree King is an assignment editor at KDPX-TV in St. Louis, MO. She dispatches a team to wherever breaking news happens. Her focus is to stay ahead of the competition. Overall, she's easy-going, respectable, and compassionate. But when it comes to dating a fellow coworker, she refuses to cross that professional line. Award-winning investigative reporter Bryan Mitchell makes life challenging for Desiree with his thoughtful gestures, sweet notes, and support. He tries to convince Desiree that as Christians, they could show coworkers how to blend their personal and private lives without compromising their morals.

In *Words of Love*, call it old fashion, but Simone French was smitten with a love letter. Not a text, email, or Facebook post, but a love letter sent through snail mail. The prose wasn't the corny roses-are-red-and-violets-are-blue stuff. The first letter contained short accolades for a job well done. Soon after, the missives were filled with passionate words from a man who confessed the hidden secrets of his soul. He revealed his unspoken weaknesses, listed his uncompromising desires, and unapologetically noted his subtle strengths. Yes, Rice Taylor was ready to surrender to love. Whew. Closing her eyes, Simone inhaled the faint lingering smell of roses on the beige plain stationery. She had a testimony. If anyone would listen, she would proclaim that love was truly blind.

In *Talk to Me*, despite being deaf because of a fireworks explosion, CEO of a St. Louis non-profit company, Noel Richardson, expertly navigates the hearing world. What some view as a disability, Noel views as a challenge—his lack of hearing has never held him back. It also helps that he has great looks, numerous university degrees, and full bank accounts. But those assets don't define him as a man who longs for the right woman in his life. Deciding to visit a church service, Noel is blind-sided by the most beautiful and graceful Deaf interpreter he's ever seen. Mackenzie Norton challenges him on every level through words and signing, but as their love grows, their faith is tested. When their church holds a yearly revival, they witness the healing power of God in others. Mackenzie has faith to believe that Noel can also get in on the blessing. Since faith comes by hearing, whose voice does Noel hear in his heart, Mackenzie, or God's?

TESTIMONY: If I Should Die Before I Wake. It is of the LORD's mercies that we are not consumed, because His compassions fail not. They are new every morning, great is Thy faithfulness. Lamentations 3:22-23, God's mercies are sure; His promises are fulfilled; but a dawn of a new morning is God' grace. If you need a testimony about God's *grace, then If I Should Die Before I Wake* will encourage your soul. Nothing happens in our lives by chance. If you need a miracle, God's got that too.

Trust Him. Has it been a while since you've had a testimony? Increase your prayer life, build your faith, and walk in victory because without a test, there is no testimony. (eBook only)

In *Her Dress*, sometimes a woman just wants to splurge on something new, especially when she's about to attend an event with movers and shakers. Find out what happens when Pepper Trudeau is all dressed up and goes to the ball, but another woman is modeling the same attire. At first, Pepper is embarrassed, then the night gets interesting when she meets Drake Logan. *Her Dress* is a romantic novella about the all-too-common occurrence—two women shopping at the same place. Maybe having the same taste isn't all bad. Sometimes a good dress is all you need to meet the man of your dreams. (eBook only)

In *Christmas Greetings*, Saige Carter loves everything about Christmas: the shopping, the food, the lights, and of course, Christmas wouldn't be complete without family and friends to share in the traditions they've created together. Plus, Saige is extra excited about her line of Christmas greeting cards hitting store shelves, but when she gets devastating news around the holidays, she wonders if she'll ever look at Christmas the same again. Daniel Washington is no Scrooge, but he'd rather skip the holidays altogether than spend them with his estranged family. After one too many arguments around the dinner table one year, Daniel had enough and walked away from the drama. As one year has turned into many, no one seems willing to take the first step toward reconciliation. When Daniel reads one of Saige's greeting cards, he's unsure if the words inside are enough to erase the pain and bring about forgiveness. Once God reveals to them His purpose for their lives, they will have a reason to rejoice.

In *Guilty of Love*, when do you know the most important decision of your life is the right one? Reaping the seeds from what she's sown; Cheney Reynolds moves into a historic neighborhood in Ferguson, Missouri, and becomes a reclusive. Her first neighbor, the incomparable Mrs. Beatrice Tilley Beacon aka Grandma BB, is an opinionated childless widow. Grandma BB is a self-proclaimed expert on topics Cheney isn't seeking advice—everything from landscaping to hip-hop dancing to romance. Then there is Parke Kokumuo Jamison VI, a direct descendant of a royal African tribe. He learned his family ancestry, African history, and lineage preservation before he could count. Unwittingly, they are drawn to each other, but it takes Christ to weave their lives into a spiritual bliss while He exonerates their past indiscretions.

In *Not Guilty*, one man, one woman, one God and one big problem. Malcolm Jamieson wasn't the man who got away, but the man God instructed Hallison Dinkins to set free. Instead of their explosive love affair leading them to the wedding altar, God diverted Hallison to the prayer altar during her first visit back to church in years. Malcolm was convinced that his woman had loss her mind to break off their engagement. Didn't Hallison know that Malcolm, a tenth-generation descendant of a royal African tribe, couldn't be replaced? Once Malcolm concedes that their relationship can't be savaged, he issues Hallison his own edict, "If we're meant to be with each other, we'll find our way back. If not, that means that there's a love stronger than what we had." His words begin to haunt Hallison until she begins to regret their breakup, and that's where their story begins. Someone must retreat, and God never loses a battle.

In *Still Guilty*, Cheney Reynolds Jamieson made a choice years ago that is now shaping her future and the future of the men she loves. A botched abortion left her unable to carry a baby to term, and her husband, Parke K. Jamison VI, is expected to produce heirs. With a wife who cannot give him a child, Parke vows to find and get custody of his illegitimate son by any means necessary. Meanwhile, Cheney's twin brother, Rainey, struggles with his anger over his ex-girlfriend's actions that haunt him, and their father, Dr. Roland Reynolds, fights to keep an old secret in the past.

In *The Acquittal*, two worlds apart, but their hearts dance to the same African drum beat. On a professional level, Dr. Rainey Reynolds is a competent, highly sought-after orthodontist. Inwardly, he needs to be set free from the chaos of revelations that make him question if happiness is obtainable. To get away from the drama, Rainey is willing to leave the country under the guise of a mission trip with Dentist Without Borders. Will changing his surroundings really change him? If one woman can heal his wounds, then he will believe that there is really peace after the storm.

Ghanaian beauty Josephine Abena Yaa Amoah returns to Africa after completing her studies as an exchange student in St. Louis, Missouri. Although her heart bleeds for his peace, she knows she must step back and pray for Rainey's surrender to Christ for God to acquit him of his self-inflicted mental torture.

In the Motherland of Ghana, Africa, Rainey not only visits the places of his ancestors, will he embrace the liberty that Christ's Blood really does set every man free.

In *Guilty by Association*, how important is a name? To the St. Louis Jamiesons who are tenth generation descendants of a royal African tribe—everything. To the Boston Jamiesons whose father never married their mother—there is no loyalty or legacy. Kidd Jamieson suffers from the "angry" male syndrome because his father was an absent in the home, but insisted his two sons carry his last name. It takes an old woman who mingles genealogy truths and Bible verses together for Kidd to realize his worth as a strong black man. He learns it's not his association with the name that identifies him, but the man he becomes that defines him.

In *The Guilt Trip*, Aaron "Ace" Jamieson is living a carefree life. He's good-looking, respectable when he's in the mood, but his weakness is women. If a woman tries to ambush him with a pregnancy, he takes off in the other direction. It's a lesson learned from his absentee father that responsibility is optional. Talise Rogers has a bright future ahead of her. She's pretty and has no problem catching a man's eye, which is exactly what she does with Ace. Trapping Ace Jamieson is the furthest thing from Talise's mind when she learns she pregnant and Ace rejects her. "I want nothing from you Ace, not even your name." And Talise meant it.

In *Free From Guilt*, it's salvation round-up time and Cameron Jamieson's name is on God's hit list. Although his brothers and cousins embraced God—thanks to the women in their lives—the two-degreed MIT graduate isn't going to let any woman take him down that path without a fight. He's satisfied with his career, social calendar, and good genes. But God uses a beautiful messenger, Gabrielle Dupree, to show him that he's in a spiritual deficit. Cameron learns the hard way that man's wisdom is like foolishness to God. For every philosophical argument he throws her way, Gabrielle exposes him to scriptures that makes him question his worldly knowledge.

In *The Confession*, Sandra Nicholson had made good and bad choices throughout the years, but the best one was to give her life to Christ when her sons were small and to rear them up in the best Christian way she knew how. That was thirty something years ago and Sandra has evolved from a young single mother of two rambunctious boys, Kidd and Ace Jamieson, to a godly woman seasoned with wisdom. Despite the challenges and trials of rearing two strong-willed personalities, Sandra maintained her sanity through the grace of God, which kept gray strands at bay.

Now, Sandra Nicholson is on the threshold of happiness, but Kidd believes no man is good enough for his mother, especially if her love interest could be a man just like his absentee father.

In *The Guilty Generation*, seventeen-year-old Kami Jamieson is so over being daddy's little girl. Now that she has captured the attention of Tango, the bad boy from her school, Kami's love for her family and God have taken a backseat to her teen crush. Although the Jamiesons have instilled godly principles in Kami since she was young, they will stop at nothing, including prayer and fasting, to protect her from falling prey to society's peer pressure. Can Kami survive her teen rebellion, or will she be guilty of dividing the next generation?

In *Fun and Games with the Jamieson Men*, The Jamieson Legacy series inspired this game book of fun activities: • Brain Teasers• Crossword Puzzles• Word Searches •Sudoku •Mazes •Coloring Pages. The Jamiesons are fictional characters that put emphasis on Black Heritage, which includes Black American History tidbits, African American genealogy, and strong Black families. Relax, grab a pencil, and play along.

In *Queen's Surrender (To a Higher Calling)*, Opposites attract...or clash. The Jamieson saga continues with the Queen of the family in this inspirational romance. She's the mistress of flirtation but Philip is unaffected by her charm. The two enjoy a harmless banter about God's will versus Queen's, who prefers her own free-will lifestyle. Philip doesn't judge her choices—most of the time—and Queen respects his opinions—most of the time. It's perfect harmony sometimes.

Queen, the youngest sister of the Jamieson clan, wears her name as if it's a crown. She's single, sassy, and most of the time, loving her status, but she's about to strut down an unexpected spiritual path. Love takes no prisoners. When the descendants of a royal African tribe on her father's maternal side show up and show off at a family game night, Queen's vanity is kicked up a notch. The Robnetts take royalty to a new level with their own Queen.

Evangelist Philip Dupree is on the hot seat as the trial pastor at Total Surrender Church. The deadline for the congregation to officially elect him as pastor is months away. The stalemate: They want a family man to lead their flock. The board's ultimatum is enough to make him quit the ministry. But can a man of God walk away from his calling?

Can two people with different lifestyles and priorities cross paths and continue the journey as one? Who is going to be the first to surrender?

THE CARMEN SISTERS SERIES

In *No Easy Catch*, Book 1, Shae Carmen hasn't lost her faith in God, only the men she's come across. Shae's recent heartbreak was discovering that her boyfriend was not only married, but on the verge of reconciling with his estranged wife. Humiliated, Shae begins to second guess herself as why she didn't see the signs that he was nothing more than a devil's decoy masquerading as a devout Christian man. St. Louis Outfielder Rahn Maxwell finds himself a victim of an attempted carjacking. The Lord guides him out of harms' way by opening the gunmen's eyes to Rahn's identity. The crook instead becomes infatuated fan and asks for Rahn's autograph, and as a good will gesture, directs Rahn out of the ambush! When the news media gets wind of what happened with the baseball player, Shae's television station lands an exclusive interview. Shae and Rahn's chance meeting sets in motion a relationship where Rahn not only surrenders to Christ, but pursues Shae with a purpose to prove that good men are still out there. After letting her guard down, Shae is faced with another scandal that rocks her world. This time the stakes are higher. Not only is her heart on the line, so is her professional credibility. She and Rahn are at odds as how to handle it and friction erupts between them. Will she strike out at love again? The Lord shows Rahn that nothing happens by chance, and everything is done for Him to get the glory.

In *Defense of Love*, Book 2, lately, nothing in Garrett Nash's life has made sense. When two people close to the U.S. Marshal wrong him deeply, Garrett expects God to remove them from his life. Instead, the Lord relocates Garrett to another city to start over, as if he were the offender instead of the victim. Criminal attorney Shari Carmen is comfortable in her own skin—most of the time. Being a "dark and lovely" African American sister has its challenges, especially when it comes to relationships. Although she's a fireball in the courtroom, she knows how to fade into the background and keep the proverbial spotlight off her personal life. But literal spotlights are a different matter altogether. While playing tenor saxophone at an anniversary party, she grabs the attention of Garrett Nash. And as God draws them closer together, He makes another request of Garrett, one to which it will prove far more difficult to say "Yes, Lord."

In *Redeeming Heart*, Book 3, Landon Thomas (In Defense of Love) brings a new definition to the word "prodigal," as in prodigal son, brother or anything else imaginable. It's a good thing that God's love covers a multitude of sins, but He isn't letting Landon off easy. His journey from riches to rags proves to be humbling and a lesson well learned. Real Estate Agent Octavia Winston is a woman on a mission, whether it's God's or hers professionally. One thing is for certain, she's not about to compromise when it comes to a Christian mate, so why did God send a homeless man to steal her heart? Minister Rossi Tolliver (Crowning Glory) knows how to minister to God's lost sheep and through God's redemption, the game changes for Landon and Octavia.

In *Driven to Be Loved*, Book 4, on the surface, Brecee Carmen has nothing in common with Adrian Cole. She is a pediatrician certified in trauma care; he is a transportation problem solver for a luxury car dealership (a.k.a., a car salesman). Despite their slow but steady attraction to each other, neither one of them are sure that they're compatible. To complicate matters, Brecee is the sole unattached Carmen when it seems as though everyone else around her—family and friends—are finding love, except her. Through a series of discoveries, Adrian and Brecee learn that things don't happen by coincidence. Generational forces are at work, keeping promises, protecting family members, and perhaps even drawing Adrian back to the church. For Brecee and Adrian, God has been hard at work, playing matchmaker all along the way for their paths cross at the right time and the right place.

In *Couple by Christmas*, five-year-old Tyler Washington wants his daddy to marry this mother. The problem is both his parents were once married, then divorced two years ago. But it's Christmas time and the holidays are not the same. This year, Derek has custody, and he knows the loneliness his ex-wife will face on Christmas Day without their son. He experienced it the previous year. His past regrets and Tyler's request have Derek thinking. Maybe, just maybe, Robyn would be willing to do things as a family again for Tyler's sake. At best, act as a couple for Christmas.

In *Prayers Answered by Christmas*, Christmas is coming. While other children are compiling their lists for a fictional Santa, eight-year-old Mikaela Washington is on her knees, making her requests known to the Lord: One mommy for Christmas please. Portia Hunter refuses to let her ex-husband cheat her out of the family she wants. Her prayer is for God to send the right man into her life. Marlon Washington will do anything for his two little girls, but can he find a mommy for them and a love for himself? Since Christmas is the time of year to remember the many gifts God has given men, maybe these three souls will get their heart s desire.

Lean on Me, Book 1. No one should have to go it alone... Caregivers sometimes need a little TLC too.

Tabitha Knicely believes in family before everything. She may be overwhelmed caring for her beloved great-aunt, but she would never turn her back on the woman who raised her, even if Aunt Tweet's dementia is getting worse. Tabitha is sure she can do this on her own. But when Aunt Tweet ends up on her neighbor's front porch, and the man has the audacity to accuse Tabitha of elder abuse, things go from bad to awful. Marcus Whittington feels a mountain of regret at causing problems for Tabitha and her great-aunt. How was he to know the frail older woman's niece was doing the best she could? As Marcus gets to know Aunt Tweet and sees how hard Tabitha is fighting to keep everything together, he can't walk away from the pair. Particularly when helping Tabitha care for her great-aunt leads the two of them on a spiritual journey of faith and surrender.

Here For You, Book 2. Rachel Knicely's life has been on hold for six months while she takes care of her great aunt, who has Alzheimer's. Putting her aunt first was an easy decision—accepting that Aunt Tweet is nearing the end of her battle is far more difficult. Nicholas Adams's ministry is bringing comfort to those who are sick and homebound. He responds to a request for help for an ailing woman but when he meets the Knicelys, he realizes Rachel is the one who needs support the most. Nicholas is charmed by and attracted to Rachel, but then devastating news brings both a crisis of faith and roadblocks to their budding relationship that neither could have anticipated. This beautifully emotional and clean story contains a hero and heroine who are better at taking care of other people than themselves, a dark moment that shakes their faith, and a well-earned happily ever after.

Stand by Me, Book 3. An uplifting story about embracing love and giving others—and yourself—one more chance

When it comes to being a caregiver, Kym Knicely has been there and done that. Then she meets Charles "Chaz" Banks and soon learns that every caregiving situation is different. Chaz takes care of his seven-year-old autistic granddaughter, Chauncy. Although Kym's attraction to Chaz is strong, she must decide whether a romantic relationship can survive and thrive between two people at different stages in life. It's a journey with a different set of rules that Kym must play by if she and Chaz are to have their happily ever after and the faith and family they envision.